Praise for Linda Ford

"A tender, sweet love story with characters who only want the best for others and themselves."
—*RT Book Reviews* on *Dakota Cowboy*

"Ford's sweet, charming love story has well-written characters that demonstrate strong faith, even though they stumble along the way."
—*RT Book Reviews* on *The Cowboy's Baby*

"*The Journey Home* is a splendid tale of love, hope and faith."
—*RT Book Reviews*

Praise for Winnie Griggs

"Griggs pens a terrific and lovely story."
—*RT Book Reviews* on *The Heart's Song*

"Griggs is a wonderful storyteller."
—*RT Book Reviews* on *The Hand-Me-Down Family*

"Griggs delivers the perfect blend of romance, adventure and laughter. Her characters are charming, quirky and unpredictable."
—*RT Book Reviews* on *The Christmas Journey*

LINDA FORD

shares her life with her rancher husband, a grown son, a live-in client she provides care for and a yappy parrot. She and her husband raised a family of fourteen children, ten adopted, providing her with plenty of opportunity to experience God's love and faithfulness. They've had their share of adventures, as well. Taking twelve kids in a motor home on a three-thousand-mile road trip would be high on the list. They live in Alberta, Canada, close enough to the Rockies to admire them every day. She enjoys writing stories that reveal God's wondrous love through the lives of her characters.

Linda enjoys hearing from readers. Contact her at linda@lindaford.org or check out her website at www.lindaford.org, where you can also catch her blog, which often carries glimpses of both her writing activities and family life.

WINNIE GRIGGS

is a city girl born and raised in southeast Louisiana's Cajun Country who grew up to marry a country boy from the hills of northwest Louisiana. Though her Prince Charming (who often wears the guise of a cattle rancher) is more comfortable riding a tractor than a white steed, the two of them have been living their own happily-ever-after for more than thirty years. During that time they raised four proud-to-call-them-mine children and a too-numerous-to-count assortment of dogs, cats, fish, hamsters, turtles and 4-H sheep.

Winnie has held a job at a utility company since she graduated from college, and saw her first novel hit bookstores in 2001. In addition to her day job and writing career, Winnie serves on committees within her church, on the executive boards and committees of several writing organizations and is active in local civic organizations—she truly believes the adage that you reap in proportion to what you sow.

In addition to writing and reading, Winnie enjoys spending time with her family, cooking and exploring flea markets. Readers can contact Winnie at P.O. Box 14, Plain Dealing, LA 71064, or email her at winnie@winniegriggs.com.

LINDA FORD
WINNIE GRIGGS

Love Inspired

Recycling programs for this product may not exist in your area.

™ LOVE INSPIRED BOOKS

ISBN-13: 978-0-373-82889-0

ONCE UPON A THANKSGIVING

www.LoveInspiredBooks.com

Printed in U.S.A.

CONTENTS

SEASON OF BOUNTY

Linda Ford

Among the things I am thankful for is my family.
Each and every one of them holds a special place
in my thoughts. This book is dedicated to them:

I am privileged to have every one of you
in my family and in my heart.
May you realize how much you are loved
and how much we have to be thankful for.

O give thanks unto the Lord; for he is good:
for his mercy endureth forever.
—*Psalms* 136:1

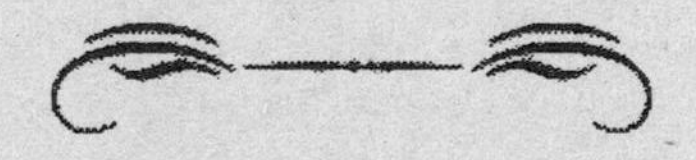

Chapter One

Hopewell, Montana
November 1890

Kathleen Sanderson cracked open the door. Before her stood a rough-looking man twisting a battered Stetson in his hands. His bent head revealed overgrown, untidy brown hair. Her glance took in the trail-worn, dusty, shearling-lined coat.

"Rosie, I know you told me to stay away, but I need your help." He raised his head to reveal demanding brown eyes that widened before they bored into Kathleen. "You're not Rosie."

"True. She's busy with the baby. If you'll wait—"

"Buck." Rosie's voice rang with shock as she joined Kathleen in the doorway. "I thought I'd made myself clear."

"I'll take the baby." Kathleen lifted nine-month-old Lilly from her mother's arms and retreated to the far end of the room, wishing the house was larger so she could escape and let these two work out their differences without her as audience. Yet this way her curiosity might be satisfied.

"Buck," Rosie continued, keeping her words low but not disguising her concern, "I told you I don't want to be associated with—" Her voice dropped to a whisper. "You know… Go away before you ruin everything."

Buck lifted his head, glanced past Rosie, saw Kathleen and shuttered his feelings, but not before she'd seen stark misery. He didn't shift his gaze away, making it impossible for her to get a satisfying breath. Then he returned his attention to Rosie and her lungs expanded with a whoosh.

"I wouldn't be here if I knew what else to do." A beat, two, in which Kathleen wondered if Rosie found his statement as demanding as she did.

"Rosie, I have a son and he's ill. I can't chase after cows or live in a bunkhouse with a sick kid. You're my sister. My only relative. Surely you'll help me for the sake of my son."

Rosie gasped. "You're married? Without even letting me know?"

"Not married. I adopted the boy. Help us?"

"I don't know." Rosie glanced over her shoulder toward Kathleen as if seeking some signal one way or the other from her.

Kathleen sensed how troubled Rosie was. Understood something about this man made her tremble.

She shifted Lilly to her hip and moved to Rosie's side to indicate her support, but it wasn't clear in her mind if she meant to encourage Rosie or her brother. "Rosie, how would you feel if it was one of your boys?" She had two—Mattie, two and a half, and Junior, four years old—who both nosed around the corner of the bedroom where they'd been playing to eye this stranger at their door.

Buck sent Kathleen a grateful glance before he appealed to Rosie. "I'd help you. You know it." The emotion in his tone caught at Kathleen's heart. A man who cared deeply. Her heart buckled and bowed with feelings she didn't recognize. Had never before in her nineteen years experienced.

Buck stepped aside. "Look at him."

A child of no more than six or seven slumped on the back of a pinto horse, wrapped up against the elements until he could barely move. Kathleen wondered for a moment if he was alive. Then he swayed, righted himself to keep from falling and lifted his face. Black eyes. A pale, thin face framed by black hair and a gray knitted hat.

"He's an Indian." Rosie's tone carried a hefty dose of disbelief and shock.

"Half-breed." The way Buck said it made Kathleen think he must have said so enough times to grow weary of making the explanation.

"You adopted him?"

Buck nodded. "I'll tell you the whole story if you let us in. He needs to be warm and dry."

Rosie rocked her head back and forth and gave careful consideration to the faces of each of her children.

"Rosie," Kathleen urged, knowing this was none of her business, yet not able to turn her back on a man and child needing help. More than that, who needed a welcome.

Not everyone would understand her concern. She knew that well enough. If her parents saw this pair on the street they would turn their backs and pretend they didn't exist. They'd rush Kathleen by and try to shield her from seeing them. Her parents had objected strenuously when Kathleen mentioned she would like to befriend Rosie.

"She's not our sort," Father said.

"The children are always grubby," Mother added, shuddering and pressing her lace-trimmed, monogrammed hankie to her nose as if the mere mention of them offended her senses.

"She's alone," Kathleen pointed out, not adding that Kathleen felt almost as alone much of the time. "Her husband is working in a logging camp and she has three little ones." At least Rosie had her babies. Kathleen had no one but Mother and Father. Not for the first time, she wondered why her friends never seemed to last. Was there something about her that made her forgettable? Or worse? Maybe she somehow, unknowingly, repelled people. "I think she appreciates me visiting." She helped as much as she could without offending Rosie.

Father studied her for a moment. "How did you meet her?"

She'd told them before but they hadn't listened. "She was leaving the store with an armload of groceries, trying to hold the baby and keep track of little Mattie, who was set on exploring the display of shovels. She dropped a letter in the confusion and I picked it up and offered to help her get home."

"She lives across town, doesn't she?"

"Yes." He knew that, too, of course. He only wanted to make sure Kathleen realized how inappropriate he considered her association with someone from the poor side of town. "She's new in Hopewell and doesn't know anyone. Everyone needs friends." Neither parent relented, but she knew exactly what to say to get their permission to visit again. "Aren't we, as Christians, commanded to welcome strangers?"

Her father's silence meant reluctant acquiescence.

She had been back several times and thought Rosie welcomed her. On her part, Kathleen enjoyed someone her age to visit with.

As she thought how they were slowly becoming friends, Rosie stood at the door, patting her fingertips together in a rapid dance. "I don't want any trouble." She flung about to stare into the center of the room. "Once people learn who Buck is and see his kid..." She didn't say what she expected would happen.

"Who is he?" Who was this man who took in a half-breed child and begged an unwelcome invitation to care for him? It made her long to enter his thoughts and explore them.

She hadn't even finished the question when he said, "I don't intend anyone should find out I'm here. I won't stay any longer than I need to. Only long enough for Joey to get his strength."

"Joey? That his name?"

Buck nodded and smiled, changing his worry into affection, and if Kathleen wasn't mistaken, a whole lot more.

She jerked her thoughts back to the present. Why did she think he seemed a loyal, committed sort of man? She didn't know anything at all about him except he faced Rosie on behalf of his sick son. But he'd informed Rosie he didn't intend to stay. Why not? She wanted to demand an answer. But it was none of her business. Just because she wanted someone…anyone…to stay in her life long-term was no reason to pin her longings on Rosie's transient brother. Poor unsuspecting man. She touched Rosie's elbow in appeal. "He needs a friend. What better friend than a sister?"

Rosie took Lilly and stepped back in silent permission.

Buck trotted to the pinto, spoke softly to the boy and lifted his arms. The child slid into them so smoothly that Kathleen caught her breath, as if feeling the weight of the youngster land against her own heart.

Kathleen opened the door wide and ushered Buck into the house. She shoved a chair closer to the stove for him to sit on.

"Thank you." Buck sounded weary and wary. No doubt he wondered who she was and what role she played. Then he gave his complete attention to Joey, slipping the heavy winter wear from him.

The boy shivered, though Kathleen knew by the

bright red spots on each cheek he was fevered. His breathing whistled in and out.

"I don't want my children sick," Rosie murmured, and backed away from the door until she reached her sons.

Buck sighed. "I'm sorry." He looked into Kathleen's eyes. "But what could I do? What would you do in the same circumstance?"

"I'd go home."

His eyes crinkled in a mixture of humor and regret. "This is the closest place to home I have."

Kathleen felt herself being drawn into something in his look. Couldn't say for certain what it was—only that it filled her with sadness that a man should not know a welcome any better than what Rosie offered. "If there's anything I can do to help…"

His smile widened and dipped into her heart. Startled at her reaction, she dropped to her knees to look more closely at his son. "Joey, I'm pleased to meet you."

Joey's unblinking gaze revealed nothing.

"My name is Kathleen Sanderson. I'm a friend of your aunt's. That's her over there, Aunt Rosie. Those are your cousins." She named them.

"Hello." Junior stepped forward, but his mother caught his shoulder and pulled him back.

Kathleen spared Rosie a moment's consideration. Shouldn't she be more charitable toward her brother and this child? If Kathleen had a brother or sister, she would do anything she could to help them. But it seemed Rosie was unaware of the blessing of a sibling.

"Never mind. They'll soon be your friends."

Joey turned his face up to ask Buck a silent question. In the moment of wordless interchange between the pair she sensed a connection, an affection needing no words, yet so evident it brought a sting to her eyes.

Buck cupped the boy's head and pressed it to his chest. "We'll be okay, little buddy."

Joey let out a sigh ending on a gasp as he fought for air.

"How long has he been ill?" Kathleen asked.

"Longer than I care to admit." Buck sat the boy up and brushed the long black hair off his face. "I haven't been fair to him, dragging him along with me. I guess I figured it was the sort of life he was born to." He shook his head. "He deserves more."

"Children get sick. It happens." She longed to reassure him. She ached to give him the welcome Rosie refused. "Now that he's here, he'll start to mend." She touched his cheeks. Hot. Dry. Parchment-paper fragile. Her knuckles brushed Buck's and she jerked back. Pushed to her feet. Turned to Rosie. "He's burning up."

"Sponge him. A good washing wouldn't likely go amiss."

"Rosie, you surprise me." Buck spoke in a flat tone.

Kathleen silently echoed his words as she prepared a basin of water.

"Take his shirt off," Rosie instructed.

Kathleen waited as Buck did so, then knelt at his

side and lifted a wet cloth. Joey shrank back, his eyes widening.

"I'll do it." Buck reached for the cloth. Again their fingers brushed. She stilled herself not to react. He paused. Slowly she lifted her head to meet his steady consideration, sat back on her heels as his look went on and on, peeling away protective layers she didn't even realize existed—layers established by her upbringing, of being sheltered to the point she often felt she was a lonely spectator of the world. Her parents had long taught her that their station in life demanded certain requirements of her. Namely, to associate only with appropriate people and marry within their circle, meaning to marry well. Yet nowhere in the approved acquaintances had she seen a man so devoted to a child not his own, from an often despised race. Nor had she ever felt a reaction that made her heart beat so erratically.

She drew back to one of the mismatched chairs around the table and watched Buck sponge Joey, murmuring softly as he worked, sometimes in foreign sounding words. All the while, Joey watched him with utmost faith.

Kathleen knew for a fact a man who could earn such trust from a child was a man worthy of the same kind of trust from others. Yet there was something about him that put Rosie on edge. What could it possibly be?

Buck wondered about the young woman watching him. She didn't seem the kind who normally hung out with Rosie, nor visited in a shack barely big enough for a family. He looked about the room. A battered wooden table. Mismatched chairs. A stove and one cupboard in the kitchen area. Beyond, a rocking chair and a small bookshelf containing two books and a basket of mending. One door next to the bookshelf where Rosie hovered, her eyes guarded. His visit would seriously crowd the place, though the floor provided more than enough room for the pair of them. In his twenty-two years he'd slept in far worse places.

Kathleen Sanderson. She'd said her name with pride and confidence of one familiar with respect. No doubt she would be shocked to learn his identity.

Nor did he intend she should. Marriage had provided Rosie with an escape and he didn't plan to ruin things for her.

Being a cowboy, moving from job to job, had given him his only escape.

Kathleen leaned forward. "He's certainly fond of you."

Buck chuckled. "He's smart enough to know where his next meal comes from."

She blinked as if startled by his frank words. Then laughed. "You're teasing, but I'd say it was more than that."

He looked at Joey who watched him with those dark, unblinking eyes of his. "We've formed a sort of mutual admiration society, haven't we, buddy?"

Joey nodded, his expression still solemn.

Buck cupped his son's head and brushed his thumb along the boy's cheeks. When had they shrunk so badly? "I'm sorry, little guy. I should have realized sooner just how sick you are."

"He needs some nourishing broth." Rosie sighed. "Guess I'll have to get some." She handed the baby to Junior. "You kids stay here and play." Then she marched toward the stove and pulled a pot forward. "Good thing for you soup is about all we eat around here."

Buck chuckled. "I knew you couldn't stay mad at me for long." He turned to Kathleen to explain. "She likes me a lot more than she lets on."

"She hides it awfully well." Her smile lit up her face, sent dancing lights into her blue eyes, riveting him motionless.

He studied her. Blond hair carefully pulled back in a wave ending in a roll at her neck. An oval face that belonged on a cameo, pretty pink lips. Everything about her said *rich, refined.*

What was she doing here?

Her cheeks blossomed rose color, and he realized he'd been staring and tore his attention away.

Rosie pulled a bowl from the cupboard and ladled in broth and bits of carrots. She set the bowl on the table. "Eat."

Joey pressed into Buck's chest. Buck understood his caution, fear even. He had plenty of reason for it. "Say 'thank you, Aunt Rosie.'"

Joey shivered. But he must learn his manners, so Buck nudged him.

"Thank you, Auntie." The boy's normally soft voice crackled from the effects of his illness.

Rosie sat across the table. "You're welcome."

Buck pulled up to the table close to Kathleen. He knew Joey wouldn't be comfortable sitting on a chair by himself, so he held him and encouraged him to eat.

"This is lots better than what I've been feeding you, isn't it, buddy?"

"I like rabbit." Joey's firm tones informed everyone where his loyalty lay, and Buck chuckled.

"You'd say that if all we ate was gopher."

"I like gopher, too."

Buck laughed and scrubbed his knuckles across the boy's head. "You ever tasted one?"

"Not yet."

Kathleen's soft laughter filled Buck's senses. My, he did like a woman with a gentle laugh. "He's determined to be loyal to you no matter what."

Buck allowed himself a glance of acknowledgment and was immediately warmed by the admiration in her eyes. "He doesn't know any better."

"Yes, I do."

Kathleen and Buck both laughed, sharing something more than enjoyment of Joey's conviction. Something he couldn't name, but it felt like a gift from God.

Strange. He hadn't thought of God, or His gifts or anything of the sort for a long time.

Rosie leaned forward on her elbows. "So how did you and Joey find each other?"

"Bless you, Rosie."

"For what?"

"For saying it like that."

She shrugged. "I have never been able to stay annoyed with you." She shifted her attention to Kathleen. "Does that make me weak?"

"No, Rosie," Kathleen said gently. "It makes you a good sister."

"She is that. We learned to stick together a long time ago, didn't we, sister?"

"Then we found out we were better off not being together." Her words contained more than a hint of warning. "Now tell us about Joey. Unless you'd rather wait."

He understood her unspoken acknowledgment that he might prefer not to speak of it in Joey's hearing. Or before her own children who hovered at the doorway, hearing and seeing everything. "He knows every detail already."

"I was there," Joey pointed out as if they might have forgotten.

Buck wished the little guy could have missed certain portions of the experience, but at least God had protected him. Again, he thought of God. Not once until now had he stopped to consider God protected Joey throughout an ordeal that might have ended much differently. Why was he suddenly realizing it?

He shifted so he could consider Kathleen out of the corner of his eyes. Something about her nudged him toward nobler, kinder thoughts than he'd enjoyed in a very long time.

What would she think after she heard Joey's story?

Would she be repulsed? Warmed? He could only hope it would give both her and Rosie a kindly disposition toward his son.

Chapter Two

Kathleen leaned close, not wanting to miss a word of Buck's explanation. Something about the fondness between Buck and Joey made her wonder if a heart could weep with emotion.

Buck settled back in his chair, a distant look in his eyes, as if he lived the past again. "It was a year ago this past spring and I was heading west. Heard a rancher out there needed a few more hands. Figured it was as good a place as any to find work. I rode up a little ridge and stopped to look around. Remember thinking the mountains made a mighty purty sight, glistening with their winter snowcaps under the bright sunshine. Then I brought my gaze closer to hand and saw what appeared to be the remains of a wagon accident. Rode on down to investigate." He paused and swallowed hard.

Kathleen guessed what he'd found had been unpleasant.

"A man and his wife had been killed."

"Bad man shoot Mama and Papa," Joey said, his voice betraying a thread of sorrow.

"The woman was Indian, the man appeared to be a white miner. I gave them a decent burial and marked the place with fragments of their wagon. There were no papers, no identification. Everything had been picked through and scattered."

"Man look for Papa's money. Find it. Steal it." As Joey listed the deeds he kept his attention on his bowl of soup, though he no longer lifted the spoon to his mouth.

Buck squeezed the back of Joey's neck and the boy relaxed visibly. "I knew from the things left that a child had been with them. I hated the thought the murderers had taken him. It was late in the day so I made camp, intending to resume my journey in the morning. During the night I heard something or someone, but the intruder was gone as fast as he came."

"I was hungry," Joey explained.

Buck chuckled. "When I got up I knew no critter had been in my camp. Only things missing were biscuits and beans. So I hunkered down over my breakfast and studied the tracks. Knew it was a child. Guessed it was the one who'd been on the wagon."

"I hide from bad man. Hide from Buck, too. I not know he not be a bad man."

"Took me a few days to prove it. Then I headed to the nearest town. No one knew the dead family. No one knew Joey. He didn't know of any family but his ma and pa. The sheriff made inquiries. But nothing. I asked the preacher what I should do and he said, why not adopt him? So I did."

The way he grinned gave Kathleen an emptiness, as if her life lacked something. She tried valiantly to dismiss the feeling. After all, what could her life be lacking? Her parents provided her with everything she needed. She had been at finishing school getting a privileged education until her mother's illness required she return home to help care for her. As soon as her mother felt better, she'd return to the Eastern college. She hadn't been there long enough to make friends, but when she got back she would. God willing, she'd find a friend who would remain loyal throughout their years at college.

Above and beyond that, she had a living relationship with God. Had never doubted His love and care. Still, had she ever done anything half as noble as Buck had? Had she ever loved anyone like Buck loved Joey? Had she ever been loved like that? Yes, her parents loved her, she had no doubt, but it seemed their love carried heavy expectations.

Buck watched her. His eyes revealed understanding. Warmth.

As if he read her thoughts.

She ducked her head, amazed at how foolish she proved to be. Until this moment she considered herself a commonsense person who didn't think or act rashly.

"Buck my papa." Joey sounded so proud, Kathleen's throat tightened.

She dare not look at Buck again, afraid of the way

her emotions clogged her heart. Instead, she glanced at Rosie. When she saw the same glisten of tears in her eyes she felt in her own, she sniffed.

"Yes, I am. And you're my son. Forever and always."

Kathleen couldn't breathe. Couldn't think beyond the stuffiness in her nose. Never before had she known such open affection between a man and his son…his adopted son, though she guessed he wouldn't acknowledge any distinction. He seemed such a decent man.

Rosie blew her nose on a hankie. "You're a good man, Buck, but it doesn't change anything."

Kathleen couldn't imagine why Rosie was so fearful.

"I'm well aware of it. I'm only here until Joey is better."

At that moment, Joey's head nodded. Buck caught him before he planted his face in the bowl of soup. He lifted the boy, tossed his coat on the floor in the corner and was about to put Joey there.

Kathleen gave Rosie a hard look. "Are you going to let him sleep on the floor? The boy is sick. Besides—" she lowered her voice "—don't you think he's been through enough?"

Rosie lifted her hands in a sign of defeat. "I give up. Buck, use the room past the stove. It's our bedroom, but I can't bring myself to sleep there with Bill gone."

Buck jerked to full attention. "He's gone? How

long ago?" He shifted his gaze to the children who played in the doorway.

"He left a few weeks ago to work in a logging camp. We came here expecting a job but it fell through. We can't live in the camp so Bill left us here." She glanced about. "This is a nice, solid little house."

Buck let out a noisy gust. "I thought you meant he was gone…gone for good, as in…well, you know."

Rosie grinned widely. "If you could see the look on your face…" She tipped her head back and looked pleased with herself. "I have to admit I enjoyed that. Sort of evens us up for you showing up at my door."

Kathleen couldn't read the look the two exchanged. Sharing a secret. She felt she intruded into their lives without invitation. She envied them their obvious affection. She wondered if they realized how blessed they were to have each other and their children.

"Consider us even, then. I'm happy to let you do so." Buck shouldered his way into the room. A cold draft blasted through the kitchen.

Junior waited until Buck was out of sight. "Mama, do we have to stay here forever?"

Rosie crossed the room and took Lilly. "Come on over. It will soon be time for supper."

Kathleen glanced out the window. Long shadows slanted across the skiff of snow. She jumped to her feet. "I've stayed far too long. Mother will be worrying." Her coat hung near the stove and she shrugged into it, pulled on her fur hat and mittens.

Buck stood in the bedroom doorway, watching.

She felt his measured consideration. Determined to ignore him, she turned to Rosie instead. "I could come back tomorrow." Perhaps Rosie wouldn't welcome her company as eagerly now that her brother was there. "If you want."

Rosie's lips flattened. "Nobody's forcing you to come."

Kathleen refused to be offended by the woman's remarks. In the few weeks she'd been visiting, she'd learned Rosie didn't expect any offers of friendship. But Kathleen didn't intend to be a fair-weather friend. She patted Rosie's shoulder. "I only asked because I thought you might enjoy spending time alone with your brother." For some insane reason her cheeks warmed. She could well imagine such pleasure.

Rosie nodded. "I'm sorry for being prickly. It's just…" She darted a look toward Buck. The pair sent wordless messages to each other, then Rosie shrugged. "I'd be pleased if you'd come again."

Kathleen understood Rosie's caution. She, too, had learned to wonder if a friend would visit again. "I'll be back. After all, we have that quilt to work on." She'd noticed a shortage of warm bedding and offered to help Rosie sew a quilt. Rosie had scraps of material and Kathleen intended to supply a woolen batt.

Only when she reached the outer door did she allow herself to look directly at Buck. "It was nice meeting you, Mr.—" She realized he'd never given his surname.

He grinned. "Buck is name enough for me."

"Nice meeting you, Buck." She knew she blushed to speak so familiarly. Her parents would be shocked.

"My pleasure, Miss Sanderson."

The way he said it made her cheeks grow even warmer.

She scurried out and rushed toward home. When had she ever had such a reaction to any man? Never. But then she'd never before met such a cowboy, never seen such a kind smile. Her feet slowed. What was she thinking?

Nothing. Nothing at all, except it would be nice for Rosie to have a man around to take care of filling the wood box and fetching water.

It would be equally as nice for Buck to have a place to care for his son.

Her parents both sat in the drawing room and glanced up as Kathleen hurried in, rubbing her hands together to ease the chill.

"You're very late," Mother said. "I was beginning to worry."

Father lowered the papers he'd been reading and studied Kathleen. "I'm still not comfortable with you going to that woman's shack. It's in a rough area of town. You aren't safe."

Kathleen held back annoyance at their continued resistance to her being friends with Rosie. "There is no danger." For some reason, Buck's image flitted through her mind. There was something about him his sister considered threatening, but she couldn't imagine it was the kind of danger her father meant. "Rosie and her children are very nice people. You would like them if you ever got to know them."

Mother fluttered her hand. "That's not likely to ever happen, is it? We simply don't belong in the same circles."

Kathleen had invited Rosie to attend church with her. Assured her she would be welcome. "I would think rich and poor are both welcome in the church."

"Why, of course they are." But Rosie heard her unspoken qualifier—*just don't expect us to sit in the same pew.*

Having no desire to argue with them or upset them, Kathleen let the topic end. She sank to an ottoman at her mother's knees and took her hands. "How have you been this afternoon?"

"I've managed to sit up and read a bit." Mother's voice quavered. "I'm sure I'm getting stronger."

Father set aside his papers. "Kathleen, I should think you could see your mother needs your care. I don't like you neglecting her when she's not well."

Stung by his criticism, Kathleen remained on the stool beside her mother. "Mother sleeps much of the afternoon. I only intend to be gone during that time."

He glanced at the big grandfather clock ticking out the seconds in demanding rhythm.

"Today was different. Rosie's brother and his little boy showed up, and the time simply slipped away on me."

Father leaned forward in his chair. "A brother? Good. He can take care of his sister and you can find a more suitable pastime." He sat back, satisfied life would fit into his sense of right and order.

"Father, I promised her I would help her sew a quilt. I told her I would return tomorrow. I hope you won't say I can't go." She couldn't imagine returning to the boredom of sitting quietly in an armchair reading as her mother slept.

Father tapped his knee and considered her. "You used to be such an obedient child. I should never have sent you East to that college. They've filled your head with all sorts of radical ideas. I'm glad you've had cause to return home. Given time, I expect you will come to your senses." He flipped the paper in front of his face, signaling he'd spoken his last word on the subject.

Kathleen eased a sigh of relief over her teeth. At least he hadn't forbidden her to return, which left her free to do so. In the future, she would simply return before the afternoon was spent.

She schooled herself not to smile with anticipation of a visit the next day. Nor would she admit, even to herself, that it was the thought of seeing Buck again that brought the smile to her lips.

She only wanted to assess if the affection she'd witnessed was as evident as she remembered. And check if Joey was feeling better.

Buck sponged Joey several more times and fed him more broth throughout the evening. For now he seemed to be sleeping peacefully.

Rosie glanced in on them. "Likely all he needs is a warm bed and decent food."

"I hope you're right." If anything happened to the boy— "I've grown to love him more than I imagined possible."

"It's pretty obvious." She remained in the doorway. "Care to join me for tea?"

He draped an arm across her shoulders. "Just like old times?"

She patted his hand. "Buck, I'd just as soon forget about old times, if you don't mind."

"Yeah. Me, too." They sat across from each other, nursing warm cups of steaming tea. "So who is this Kathleen Sanderson and why is she visiting you?"

Rosie bristled. "What? I'm not fit for the likes of her to cross my threshold?"

He chuckled. "Is that what you think?"

"Sometimes."

"Guess we've both got reason to consider others think that very thing. So who is she and why is she here?"

"Kathleen's father is the richest man in town."

A punch of alarm raced up Buck's spine. Rich men with beautiful daughters were the worst sort. They didn't want the likes of Buck to even be in the same town. "If her father learns who I am…"

"And who I am." Her gaze bored into his—angry at his visit to her home. "You should never have come here. You promised you wouldn't."

"It's only for Joey and then I'll be gone." He glanced about the house. There were days he wished he didn't have to keep on the move. But wishing didn't change the facts. "I'll do my best to keep our secret from Kathleen. I can think of no reason she'd suspect who I am. Why should anyone be suspicious of your brother visiting? Your married name gives no clue as to who we are." He didn't want to think about his past. "Tell me how you met her."

"The Sandersons live in a big house. Even have a cook and housekeeper. Can you imagine paying someone to clean your house? 'Course, it's a mighty big house and dust probably isn't allowed to settle for even a minute. Someday I'm going to ask Kathleen how many rooms there are."

Buck sighed. Seemed he was going to get a detailed description of the house before she explained about Kathleen.

She must have guessed at his impatience. "Won't likely ever see inside the place, now will I?" She shrugged. "Not that it matters. I'm happy enough here, and Kathleen doesn't seem to mind how small and mean my house is." She told about Kathleen helping her home one afternoon as she struggled to corral young Mattie. "Since then she visits me, plays with the kids. Even helps with the dishes if they aren't done when she gets here. Now she says she wants to help me make a quilt for the children." She rocked her head back and forth. "I just don't understand why."

"Have you asked her?"

"I did. All she said was she couldn't bear the thought of me living on the edge of town with no friends. Though from what she says, I think she's as lonely as I am. She'd like me to go to church with her but I can't. If I let myself care about people and what they think, it only hurts the more when they discover the truth." Her eyes hardened. "Someone is likely to, now that you're here. Once they realize our father was—" She clamped her lips together as tears swelled in her eyes.

He filled in the blank she'd left. "A murderer." Saying the word forced him back to reality. "Don't worry. I won't be around long enough for anyone to take notice." Though he wished things could be different. Wished he could offer Joey a real home. Wished he could belong somewhere. With someone. A forbidden dream flashed through his thoughts of home and a woman. He'd had the thought before, and always the woman was faceless. Just a presence. But this time she had a face and voice…those of Kathleen Sanderson. "I will leave as soon as Joey is rested. Before people find out and drive us out of town." He knew his voice had grown hard. Rosie would understand why. They shared a secret with the power to destroy their lives. He understood why Rosie would be cautious about making friends. A person needed to be able to leave when the time came with no regrets, no glancing back over one's shoulder.

Yet he rose the next morning wondering if Kathleen would return as she had promised Rosie.

Rosie noticed how many times he glanced out the window and laughed. "She won't be along for a bit. She never comes until after lunch when her mother is napping."

"I wasn't looking for her."

"Sure you were."

"Only because I wondered if she would come as she promised."

Rosie grew serious. "I always wonder the same thing, but every time she's said she'd come, she has."

Joey sat at the table spooning in thin porridge. "Buck, who you waiting for?"

He turned away from the window. "Nobody. Just checking the weather."

Rosie snorted. "She's not your sort."

"No one is." They both knew what he meant, and he sat at the table to consider his two nephews. Sturdy-looking boys. Made Joey look as thin as he was. "Your boys appear well fed."

"Bill left us with adequate supplies. He'll send money from time to time. We won't go hungry."

"Didn't think we were, either."

"I not hungry." Joey put his spoon down as if to prove he only ate because the food was before him.

Buck smiled. He appreciated Joey's devotion, but not to the extent of him choosing to go hungry. "Finish it up."

Joey hesitated only a moment before returning his attention to the food.

Rosie stood beside Buck. "He seems a little better today."

"I hope so."

But an hour later, after playing with Mattie and Junior, Joey curled up on the floor, exhausted. Buck carried him to bed and sat at his side, watching him.

Surely he would regain his strength in a day or two and they could move on. But to where? And what did it matter? One place was the same as the next.

Joey slept through a lunch of soup and freshly baked bread. He was still asleep when a gentle knock sounded.

Buck sat at the table pretending a great interest in the pencil Junior had given him to sharpen, but every sense tingled with awareness as Kathleen stepped into the house, laughing about the wind tugging at her fine woolen coat. She shrugged out of it and hung it on a nail. "Hello, everyone." She smiled at Rosie who held Lilly, leaned over and kissed the baby's cheek, squatted to kiss Mattie's forehead, hugged Junior and then finally lifted her attention to Buck. "Hello to you, too."

"You're a breath of sunshine." He hadn't meant to sound so adoring. He only meant she made everyone smile with her greeting.

Her cheeks flushed a very becoming pink, reminding him of summer sunrises. "I'm just passing on my own feelings of happiness."

Rosie waggled her hand toward Buck. "He meant it as a compliment." She gave Buck a scolding look. "We're all glad to have you visit." Silently she warned Buck not to ruin things for her. As if his very presence wasn't enough to do that.

"I'm relieved to hear it." Kathleen glanced about. "Where's Joey?"

"Still sleeping." Worry grabbed his gut. "He's been sleeping a long time." He rushed into the bedroom, pressed his hand to the boy's forehead, but even without feeling his hot skin he knew the boy was again fevered. "I hoped he was getting better."

Rosie brought in a basin of water, and both women hovered at the bedside while Buck stripped the boy to the waist and sponged him.

"I don't think this is a good sign," Rosie murmured. "Fevers that return every day generally mean something like lung fever."

"No." Buck wouldn't allow it. "He's just run down. He'll be fine."

"Let's pray for God to strengthen his little body." Kathleen reached for Rosie's hand.

Buck understood Rosie's hesitation. Hadn't their ma prayed for God to intervene? It hadn't happened. Instead she'd died, and he and Rosie had been on their own. But for Joey, his son, he'd storm the gates of heaven if he must. He reached for Kathleen's hand, saw her start with surprise and likely shock, and he pulled back. But she reached out and clasped his hand on one side and Rosie's on the other. From her flowed confidence and faith that poured into his heart. God could heal his boy. He knew it. He believed it. He bowed his head.

"Dear Heavenly Father." Kathleen's voice rang with love and joy. "You love us so much. You are the great healer. Touch Joey. Stop the fever. Show us what part we need to play, that Your name might be glorified. Amen."

He pulled his hand to his knee, kept his head tilted

down. He'd never heard such a simple prayer, and yet he felt he had stepped into the throne room of God.

He picked up the wet cloth and continued to sponge Joey. But no longer did his spirit fret.

The fever slowly abated as it had done before. He almost dared believe this might be the last time.

Joey opened his eyes and smiled. "Hi, Buck."

"Hi, buddy. How you feeling?"

"Maybe a little hungry."

Buck's laugher was joined by Rosie's and Kathleen's. "Surely he's on the mend." He turned and gripped Kathleen's shoulder. "Thanks to you."

"No." She shook her head. "Thanks to God." Her look of assurance filled him with a sense of wonder. God actually might care about him. Amazing. Or was it only Joey God cared about?

It was a question he didn't care to answer at the moment.

Chapter Three

Kathleen couldn't believe her boldness at taking Buck's hand to pray. Praying came naturally enough to her. But what made her think it required holding a hand as solid and firm as the ground beneath her feet? Her palm still felt warmer than normal.

But she had no doubt God intervened for Joey's improvement and would continue to do so. She silently prayed it would accomplish much more…that Rosie and Buck would find healing for whatever made them so fearful and kept them away from each other.

Joey ate a bowl of soup, played with the toys for a few minutes, then crawled into Buck's lap and closed his eyes.

Kathleen watched the play of emotions on Buck's face—worry, love, hope. He lifted his eyes to hers and allowed her to see the depth of his feelings. They caught at her heart. Then he ducked his head, pressing his cheek to Joey's black hair.

Emotion clogged Kathleen's throat. This kind of love awed her. Filled her heart with yearning.

She drew in a shaking breath, wondering at the lightness of the air she sucked in, which did little to relieve her need for oxygen.

Lilly slept in Rosie's arms. Young Mattie whined.

"I need to put the little ones down for their nap." Rosie pushed to her feet. "Come along, Junior. Time for you to have a sleep."

"Mama, I want to play with Joey."

Buck looked at his son. "I don't think Joey feels much like playing at the moment. When you wake up he'll likely be ready."

Rosie took the children to the bedroom to settle them.

Kathleen expected Buck to do the same with Joey, but he stayed seated. She forced herself to remain still, though she longed to jump to her feet and pace the room. A crack in the wooden table caught her attention and she ran a fingernail along it.

"Is he asleep?" Buck whispered.

She looked. "I would say so."

"Then I'll put him down now." He shifted the boy and carried him to the bed, covered him carefully, smoothed his hair from his forehead...all ordinary things, yet watching him made her heart ache.

He stepped back, watched his son a moment, then tiptoed from the room and pulled the door part way shut. "I didn't want to put him down until he fell asleep. Seems like the least I can give him is lots of assurance of safety." He returned to the chair he occupied previously and rubbed his hand across his face. "I fear I am an inadequate parent, but I'm all the poor little guy has."

Such hope and desperation filled his voice, she couldn't bear it. "From what I've seen, you are an excellent father. The way he adores you is proof enough."

Brown eyes met hers, brimming with hunger and longing. "Do you think so?"

He loved the boy deeply and wasn't afraid to show it. The knowledge of such love—human love—gave her the feeling she missed something vital in her life. She feared it would show in her eyes but lacked the strength to tear her gaze away. "I know so."

A slow, intense smile filled his face. "I perceive you are a most generous person in every way."

It was her turn to be surprised. "How nice of you to say so." But how could he know? He'd only just met her.

His chuckle tingled along her nerves like music rushing up her veins. "You're thinking I couldn't possibly know, seeing as we've only met. But yet, I think I am correct." He leaned closer drawing her into an intimate invisible circle including only the two of them, excluding everyone and everything else. "I know you've gone out of your way to make friends with Rosie, and I'm certain it's more than what most women in your group of friends consider ordinary."

She tried to pull her thoughts into order, but all she could think was he admired her for doing something that had indeed brought criticism from others, even beyond her parents.

"You know, I haven't given God much consideration or due in a long time. Since…well, never mind that. But from the moment I stepped through that door—" He tipped his head in the general direction. "I've thought of Him several times. I think it is due to you."

"How can that be?"

"You bring God's presence into the house."

"I—" She didn't know how to answer. "If so, then I am happy to hear it."

His soft smile thanked her. "If only more people were like you." He sat back. "Maybe you can help me."

"I will if I can." Perhaps he would ask her to assist him and Rosie in sorting out their differences.

"I'd like to know if Rosie needs anything. Is she managing okay on her own?"

Not the direction she'd hoped he'd go, but to know he cared so about others filled her with sweet admiration. "She has her hands full, especially when she goes shopping." She told about her first meeting with Rosie and how his poor sister couldn't keep a hand on everything. "Mattie saw the bucketful of shiny shovels, and I suppose he thought they would make good toys. What a clatter when the bucket tipped and they all fell to the ground. The storekeeper came rushing out to see what the racket was. I think everyone stopped what they were doing to look." She laughed. "Poor Rosie didn't think it very amusing, I'm afraid."

She thought of what Rosie really needed—to become more a part of the community instead of keeping so much to herself. But before she could voice her thought, Rosie tiptoed from the bedroom.

"Were you two talking about me?" she asked.

Buck sighed. "You were the furthest thing from my mind."

Rosie considered them suspiciously. "I heard you talking while I got the children to sleep, yet the minute I step into the room you are quiet as mice."

Buck grinned. "If you insist on knowing, I was telling her all the family secrets."

Rosie drew up hard and stared at her brother. Then she laughed, a nervous twitter of a sound. "I know you're joshing. Serves me right for being so suspicious." She turned to Kathleen. "Were you serious about helping me stitch a quilt top?"

At last, something to do with her hands so her thoughts wouldn't continually run off in silly directions. "Of course. Are you ready to get started?"

Rosie fetched a basket of fabric pieces. "I thought to make one for Junior's bed, but I don't intend to take advantage of your generosity or anything."

Kathleen rubbed her hands together. "We can do this. Do you have a pattern in mind?"

The women pulled out fabric and discussed different arrangements. Once they'd chosen a pattern, they cut out a number of squares, then Kathleen started stitching them together while Rosie continued cutting.

"Where did you spend Thanksgiving last year?" Kathleen asked him.

Guess it was too much for Buck to think their project would keep them occupied and allow him the privilege of watching the subtle changes in Kathleen's expression as she chose colors and patterns and aligned the pieces. But he realized he didn't mind talking about the past year. In most ways it was one of the best in his life, with Joey to look after and love. "The two of us spent it in a settler's shack. The pioneer family had moved to town for the winter, and they were glad enough to have someone occupy their place." No doubt such simple accommodations were something she would not rejoice over, but he'd been grateful.

Kathleen and Rosie continued to work, but he felt their keen interest. "I really never gave Thanksgiving a thought until the owner of the place rode out with a bundle. Said his wife insisted he bring it to the two of us. I let Joey open it. You should have seen his eyes. I don't think he could remember receiving gifts before. Inside was enough turkey for the both of us and plenty of mashed potatoes and gravy. There were two oranges and a toy whistle. We had us a real good day. Just the two of us." He wasn't sure why he kept saying it was only he and Joey, except he wanted to believe it was how he wanted things to be. Even to his own ears it sounded lonely. But he really did have something to be thankful for—a little son and a warm house, even though the latter was temporary.

Thanksgiving was three weeks away. He should

be gone again by then, but only if he remained would Joey know a true family celebration. The temptation to stay was strong.

"It sounds sweet," Kathleen said, although her voice seemed tight, as if the words didn't want release.

"It sounds lonely." Rosie, as always, was bluntly honest. They studied each other. He wished he could stay awhile. Perhaps she did, too, but they both knew the risks. People were less than welcoming when they discovered whom their father was. He and Rosie had been driven from more than one place by a violent crowd.

He and Joey must move on.

Kathleen's gaze had not left him all the while he and Rosie shared their silent communication, and now he shifted and met her blue, intense look.

She smiled. "The church is having a special Thanksgiving service. There will be a community dinner to share the bounty of the year. It would be nice if you would attend. I think you'd enjoy it."

Her words fell into a silence, sending ripples through his thoughts. He hadn't been to church since Ma died. He wondered if Rosie had. He'd attended her wedding, held in the parsonage. It was the last time he'd seen her before yesterday, though he sent her an occasional letter. She wrote to him regularly so he knew she and Bill had moved to this town. Bill knew enough to keep one step ahead of the cruel truth of his wife's past. "I doubt I'll be here." Regret deepened his voice but he hoped no one would notice. "Rosie, you should go. It would be good for you and the kids."

Rosie allowed him the briefest glance, but enough for him to see her longing ran every bit as deep as his. "I'll think on it."

"I'll keep asking," Kathleen said.

Buck wondered how she managed to sound so serene, so confident. Not for the first time, and likely not for the last, he wished things could be different so he could get to know her better and discover who she really was.

It wasn't possible. He shifted his thoughts to other things. Like the children. Rosie's were happy and full of spirit. Was Joey on par with them? Was he suffering because of the way Buck lived? Not that he could do a thing to change it.

The children woke and the women put away the sewing. Rosie brought Lilly from the bedroom with her two boys following her. At the same time, Joey came from the other room. The boy's color had improved.

Rosie put Lilly in her chair and the other children sat around the table to eat bread and jam.

"Good food and rest are giving Joey back his strength," he said.

Kathleen's gentle gaze brushed him. "God has given us so many reasons to be thankful."

He nodded. She made it easy for him to believe in God's bountiful blessings.

"I must return home. I promised Mother and Father I wouldn't be as late as I was yesterday."

Buck scrambled to his feet. "I'll walk you home."

"It's not necessary."

Did he detect a hint of something in her voice he was loath to admit? Was she embarrassed to have him walk her home? "My mother, God rest her soul, would expect no less of me."

She considered him briefly then nodded. "Very well, though it really isn't necessary."

He bent to face his son. "Joey, you stay with Aunt Rosie. I'll be back in a few minutes. Okay?"

"You be back for sure?"

"For sure."

"Okay, then." He returned his attention to the slice of bread.

He slipped into his coat and buttoned it, then held the door for Kathleen, who had already said goodbye to everyone in the room. They tramped along the hardened path.

"Do you realize that's the first time I've heard mention of your mother?"

"Even the likes of Rosie and me have a mother and father, though they are both dead now." He regretted his words as soon as they were out and hoped she wouldn't ask about his father.

"I'm sorry for your loss, but you know I didn't mean you wouldn't have parents." She scowled at him, making him feel like a small boy.

"I'm sorry. Sometimes I am too defensive."

"Both you and Rosie. It's like you expect someone to kick you in the teeth for no reason."

Oh, they thought they had reason enough, but he wasn't about to tell her so.

Kathleen turned to him, her expression a mixture

of amusement and something more—perhaps regret? "Rosie's very fond of you."

"Like you said, she hides it pretty well."

Her sweet laugh filled his senses. "Tell me what it was like to have a sister growing up."

Her questions almost stopped him in his tracks. It took every bit of his well-developed self-control to move forward, to keep his voice steady, as if the memories weren't filled with a bittersweet taste. "Life was very different then. My parents were alive."

She didn't speak, and he wondered how aware she was of the tension gripping his heart.

"There was a time..." He slowed his words to cover his regret. "When my father laughed with joy and said we had much to be grateful for." How quickly his attitude had changed.

"It sounds nice."

"It was." How long since he'd remembered those better days? Far too long. And he vowed right there in the middle of the trail he would give Joey some memories of good times, and he'd find a way to remind Rosie of those happier days when being thankful didn't require an effort.

"Having a sibling is special."

Did he detect a lonesome note in her voice? He couldn't think it was true. She came from a secure, stable, safe family.

They passed the business section of town and climbed a slight hill to a cluster of large houses.

Kathleen stopped walking. "This is where I live." She indicated a house dominating those around it.

The place was huge. Buck could see why they might need someone to dust and clean. "Just you and your parents live here?" He failed to keep awe from his voice.

"Our cook has quarters here, too."

"Oh, then that explains why you need such a large house."

She grinned. "You know it doesn't. We don't need a big house, but my father thinks it's in keeping with his station in life." Her smile seemed slightly lop-sided. "My father has very well-formed ideas of right and wrong."

"And always does what is right?"

"Always."

"That's something to be grateful for, isn't it?" He knew his voice revealed far more than he wanted to. If his own father had always done what was right, not let his anger and frustration drive him to taking things into his own hands in such a gruesome manner...well, his life and Rosie's—and now their children's—would be much different.

Aware that she watched him closely, likely won-dering why he seemed so vehement about the idea of right and wrong when they'd been talking about her big house, he again studied the mansion before him. Lots of red brick and white trim around the seemingly endless windows on both the ground floor and second story. "It certainly makes a person stand up and take notice."

"It's just a house. Isn't a house the place where

family gathers? Seems to me that what's important. Not the size of the dwelling."

He couldn't take his eyes off the house in front of them. "If you say so."

"I do. Now stop staring at it. You're making me uncomfortable."

He jerked his attention away and toward her. "Why would it make you uncomfortable?"

"Because I don't want to be judged by who my father is or how large the house I live in is. I want to be judged for my own actions." Her words rang with fierceness.

"I wish I could think such was possible." But people would always judge him by who his father was. He couldn't imagine it would be any different for Kathleen, though for vastly different reasons.

She studied him, her gaze searching out hidden meanings in his words, secrets buried deep in his heart. "Can it not be so between us, at least?"

Her question begged so many things from him. Acceptance of her friendship, but more. Openness, sharing of secrets. He couldn't offer what she silently asked for, though he ached to do so. "I wish things could be different."

"Can't you make them so?"

"I can't control what others say or think or do."

"But you can choose who and what you are."

He searched her frank open gaze. He wanted to point out it was easy for her to choose her own path with the protection of her father's name. But he didn't want to spoil the moment.

She continued to study him. "Haven't you done that already to some extent?"

He didn't understand. His choice was to leave before people learned the truth or immediately after they did.

She must have seen his confusion. "Adopting Joey."

"That has never been a hardship." Though partly because Joey fit into Buck's way of life…moving on before people got too critical. But was he doing the child a disservice by constantly moving?

"I must go inside." Kathleen shifted her attention to the house.

"Good afternoon. Thanks for everything."

She turned back to him. Made him happy he'd said something to accomplish that. "For what?"

"For visiting Rosie and being her friend. For praying for Joey. Reminding me of God." *For being Kathleen and sharing your joy.*

She lowered her eyes. "You're welcome." Brought her gaze back to his, smiling widely. "I hope you think about God more often now."

"I surely shall." Every time he thought of Kathleen and he knew that would be often.

"Goodbye now. I'll see you tomorrow." She headed up the brick sidewalk, paused at the door to give a little wave.

He lifted a hand in response, waited until the door closed behind her then headed back to Rosie's, Kathleen's promise ringing in his ears. *See you tomorrow.*

How many tomorrows dare he plan?

He clamped his jaw down hard, making his teeth ache. Not nearly enough.

Chapter Four

Kathleen leaned against the door and waited for her heart to calm. He admired her. Approved of her friendship with Rosie. Of course he would, Rosie being his sister. But his approval meant more to her than she could explain.

She hung her coat on the hall tree and slipped out of her boots into a pair of fur-lined slippers. Central heating filled the whole house with welcoming warmth. Yes, she was grateful for the comforts of her life. Yes, she admired her parents for their moral strength. But some days it all felt hollow, and today was one of those times.

"I'm in here," Mother called from the sitting room.

Kathleen took a deep, calming breath and scolded herself for feeling so restless when she was so blessed. She stepped into the room. "Mother, you're up already. How are you?"

"I do believe I am feeling better every day." She

sighed in such a way that Kathleen wondered at the truth of her words. "I get tired of being tired."

Kathleen sat on the stool at her knees. "You did something different with your hair."

"Jeannie offered to brush and style it." Jeannie was more than housekeeper. She often did little things to brighten Mother's day. Kathleen would be sure to thank her later.

"It's very becoming."

Mother brushed her hand over her hair. "Who was that young man?"

Kathleen stalled. She didn't want her parents to know too much about Buck, aware they would heartily disapprove of Joey. "That's Rosie's brother I told you about. He insisted on seeing me safely home."

"I see." Mother studied her a long moment. "And yet you've gone back and forth safely the past few weeks."

"I assured him I didn't need an escort, but he insisted his mother would expect him to do so."

"Where is his mother?"

"She's passed away."

"Oh, I am sorry."

Kathleen wished she could talk to her mother about the thousand thoughts racing through her head. Why were Rosie and Buck so secretive? Both parents were dead. How long ago? Was Joey truly on the mend? If he was, would Buck be on his way? Why did the idea tangle her thoughts? What did it all mean? But aware her mother would tell her to forget such people, she didn't voice any of her questions. "I'll go see if Cook needs help." She hurried to the kitchen before her mother could say anything.

But Cook had everything competently under control and allowed her only to finish setting the table. Kathleen did so and stood back to study the formal dining room with its perfectly matched chairs and perfectly matched china and silver. It was all very nice but lacked something that seemed to abound around Rosie's table. Funny—she hadn't been so acutely aware of it until a day or two ago.

When Buck and Joey showed up. When she discovered in her heart an emotion she couldn't name.

Kathleen's father came in, greeted her mother and asked, "Is Kathleen home?"

She hurried from the dining room. "I'm here, Father."

"Good. Good." He settled down with the paper. "I don't want you spending all afternoon at that woman's place."

"Her name is Rosie Zacharias and she is a very nice woman, as you would surely know if you ever visited her."

Father looked over the top of his paper at Kathleen's tone. She instantly repented of her peevishness. "I only meant she's a good mother and a decent person."

Neither parent said a thing, but Kathleen knew she had shocked and disappointed them with her attitude. She had no wish to be disrespectful. In the future she must guard her thoughts and her tongue.

* * *

The hours dragged the next morning as Kathleen helped her mother sort through letters from family members. For some reason Mother enjoyed reading them over and over and putting them in chronological order. "I'm sure some day these will constitute a valuable family history."

Kathleen restrained herself from saying she wondered who would be interested in the chitchat, gossipy things most of the aunts and cousins related. "Today I wore a new chiffon dress. You would love it. Palest blue. One of your favorite colors, as I recall." "I think I neglected to tell you Mamie and Fred have been seen together more often than not. Why, I myself saw them rowing on the lake Sunday." Kathleen had no idea who Mamie and Fred were, or why anyone should care if they went out together in a rowboat.

She sighed at her frustration. Perhaps she was only being petty because she didn't have anyone who would take her out in a boat, which wasn't exactly true. Young Merv, who worked with Father, would surely take her out if she offered him any encouragement. Perhaps not in a boat, though, as there wasn't a decent lake nearby and she didn't fancy a long ride with him to get to one. She secretly thought the man a little too impressed with himself to be interesting.

He never showed the kindness to others that Buck did. Nor the approval Buck had expressed to her yesterday afternoon.

Finally Kathleen's father arrived home for lunch, again taken in the dining room. As soon as they finished and he returned to work, Mother went to lie down. At last Kathleen could don her winter outerwear and hurry to visit Rosie.

The house rang with laughter as she stepped inside. Buck was on all fours on the floor, playing horsey to three boisterous boys.

Mattie tumbled off and pulled the others with him. They landed in a giggling heap. Buck corralled the trio and tickled them. They escaped to tackle him.

Rosie held young Lilly as she watched. Kathleen stood beside her and grinned at the roughhousing.

"They've missed Bill. He played with them," Rosie said.

Kathleen tried to remember if she'd ever played with her father. She recalled only sedate walks during which she held his hand and flashed shiny new shoes. If not for the children of a large family—the Rempels—who lived a few blocks away, she wondered if she would even know what play was. Mary Rempel had been her best friend. Kathleen remembered afternoons of giggling and boisterous games and a pretend house in the bushes of the backyard. When the family moved away, Kathleen knew unabated loneliness until she went to a private girls' school. But even then, her friendships proved transitory. Again, she wondered if it was her fault. Was she lacking some necessary social skill?

Buck rolled to his back, saw Kathleen watching him and grew still, his eyes flashing such warmth and welcome she forgot to breathe. "Hi," he said. The word seemed to come from deep inside his chest.

Was it her imagination that made her think he silently invited her into a special world shared with him?

Of course it was. She gave herself a mental shake. “Everyone seems to be having a fine time.”

“It won’t last,” Rosie predicted. “Not this close to nap time.”

Mattie rolled into Junior, and right on cue they started to cry.

“Come on, you two.” Rosie led the way to the bedroom. “Bedtime.”

Buck sat up on the floor and pulled Joey into his arms. “What do you say, little buddy? Time for a rest?”

Joey pressed his head to Buck’s shoulder. “I sleep here?”

Buck nodded. “For a little while, though I think I’ll sit in a chair if you don’t mind.”

“I not mind.”

Cradling the boy, he plunked himself on a kitchen chair.

Kathleen realized she still wore her coat and slipped it off. She sat across the table from Buck as Joey’s eyes slowly closed. Watching the two of them brought a sting of tears to the back of her nose. “I think he’s asleep,” she whispered.

Buck nodded. “He’s still not up to his normal self.” He held the boy a moment longer, then laid him on the bed and covered him before he returned to the kitchen.

She sewed together more quilt pieces and tried not

to be aware of his presence. Yet she couldn't stop her eyes from glancing at him.

He leaned his elbows on the table, rested his chin in his palms and studied her so intently she ducked her head and concentrated on taking a small, even stitch.

"Tell me how you celebrate Thanksgiving in your house."

She drew in a steadying breath, grateful for the offer of normal conversation. "I love Thanksgiving. I didn't always. We have a formal meal, sometimes with guests." Mostly they were business associates and not exactly fun company for a young girl. "The mealtimes were often a bit dreary, but since the church started holding a special service with guest speakers and a shared meal, I've loved the day. More and more I appreciate how much God has blessed all of us." Her hands grew still as she sought for words to explain what she meant. "I am in awe of how much God loves us that He sent his son to earth as a baby. Can you imagine sending Joey into a place where you knew he would be shunned and tortured?"

Bleakness filled Buck's face, and she wished she hadn't used his son as an example. She tended to forget he was mixed-race and likely faced prejudice.

"Good reason to spend winters in isolated shacks, wouldn't you say?"

She didn't think so, but how could she explain in such a way she wouldn't be misunderstood? "What I see between you and Joey," she began slowly, forming her thoughts as she spoke, "is a wonderful example of fatherly love and care. I'm convinced you would do anything for his well-being. I think by hiding your relationship, by seeking isolation, you deprive others of witnessing such a fine example. Our society is the poorer for the loss." She could think of nothing more to add, though the words were inadequate for the emotion she tried to convey.

Buck stared at her, swallowed hard. "You make me want to walk boldly into the town's businesses with Joey at my side."

"There's no reason you shouldn't." But was it for his sake and Joey's she wanted him to believe so? Or for her own sake? She let a picture form in her mind of Buck openly being her friend.

"Life isn't so simple for everyone." His expression grew hard, guarded. Again, the evidence of a secret. She wanted to ask him about it, but Rosie returned and took up needle and thread.

For the next few days, the afternoons passed in the same fashion with the exception that Buck didn't give her an opportunity to say anything more about walking openly and proudly down the street. Kathleen prayed he would believe he could do so or that she would get a chance to discuss it again, because every day she discovered something more she liked and admired about this man—his easy laughter when he played with the children, the way he sprang to his feet to help Rosie. And herself. She ducked her head over her sewing to hide the heat in her cheeks as she thought of how he lifted her coat from her shoulders and hung it on the rack. A common courtesy, yet when his fingers brushed her neck her reaction was far from common. The way her heart lurched against her rib cage made it impossible to think.

Each afternoon, he escorted her home.

"Won't you come in and meet Mother?" she asked on this particular day—a request she'd considered several times before, but because of her uncertainty as to how Mother would react, she'd never yet voiced it. Now she wanted nothing more than for Buck and Mother to meet.

"I don't think it would be wise," Buck said, his expression giving away nothing.

"I think you'd enjoy meeting my mother. And she you."

He shook his head. "There are things you don't know about me. No one here does. Best to keep it that way."

"I wish you'd tell me what they are so I could understand." She didn't care that her request made it sound like she had a right to know, which she didn't—except for the fact that she admired him and cared how he seemed to feel, he must remain an outsider.

A gentle smile lifted his lips and softened his gaze. "Maybe I will some time." Hardness returned so fast, she almost gasped. "You do realize I promised Rosie I wouldn't hang about until people noticed me. I think I am perilously close to reaching that place."

She reached for his arm, stopped herself before she touched him. "You won't suddenly disappear without a word, will you? I've had friends that dropped out of my life like that. I—" Why did she think it would matter how it had shattered her life? But she steadied her voice and continued. "I found it hard to accept. I asked myself all sorts of questions. Was it my fault? Was there something wrong with me? Wasn't I worthy of their friendship?"

His smile touched her. "Kathleen, anyone would be honored to be your friend."

Her thoughts skidded to a halt as his words spread like wildfire through her insides. Honored? Could he possibly mean it?

"I'll tell you before I leave. I promise."

She nodded and relaxed. She had a strong feeling that a promise from Buck was as good as money in the bank. "I'll see you tomorrow, then?"

"I'll be there."

She hurried into the house, a smile curving her lips. How sweet to know he would be there tomorrow. If only she could persuade him to consider more. More than that, he made her believe her lack of friends wasn't due to some flaw in her makeup.

Mother greeted her in the hall. "It's not proper for you to visit a man on the street like that."

"Mother, I wasn't doing anything wrong."

"He's below you." Mother made it sound like Buck belonged in the gutter.

"He's a decent man." Stilling defensive words on Buck's behalf, she hung her coat on the rack, glad of the excuse to avoid meeting her mother's gaze. "Just as his sister is a decent woman."

"Your father and I don't approve of how much time you're spending with this family."

"Mother, I am only extending Christian kindness in a way I feel I should." Yet it was as much for her sake as for theirs that she went. Having Rosie and Buck as friends eased her loneliness. But only one argument would convince Mother. "Jesus didn't make a distinction between the rich and the poor."

"He was God. You are just a woman."

"I can't believe you said that." She slowly faced her mother. "I don't think my being a woman has anything to do with extending friendship to others." Was it only friendship she longed for from Buck? Or did something deeper, wider, more intense beckon? Afraid her cheeks would flash guilty color, she ducked her head to dust her skirt. Friendship was a good start, but she allowed herself to acknowledge she wanted more.

Buck, with his easy love for Joey, Rosie and her children, and with his loyalty to what he believed, filled in the hollow spots in her heart simply by being there.

If only he would stop believing he had to leave.

"Your father is right. That Eastern college has given you strange ideas."

"No, Mother. Reading God's word—" learning to think for herself "—has given me these ideas, and I'd hardly call them strange." She slipped her arm through her mother's. "Now let's not argue. Tell me what you've been doing. Did you finish going through your letters?"

Mother sniffed then brightened at the chance to talk about what she'd done. "I finished them and started to answer some I've neglected. I haven't seen some of these dear people since before you were born, but I don't want to lose contact."

Kathleen encouraged her mother to talk and tried to still the little annoyance that she felt more regard for people whom she hadn't seen in twenty years or so than she did for those who lived only a few blocks away.

Later that night, after she'd gone to bed, she heard her parents talking and guessed she was the subject of their long discussion. She fully expected one of them to insist on her ending her visits to Rosie's. But after lunch the next day, her mother wiped her arm across her eyes in a gesture of weariness and waved her away. "Do what you want. I need to have a nap."

Thankful to be free to continue her visits, Kathleen slipped away.

Joey was stronger, ready to travel. Still Buck made no plans to leave. He couldn't bring himself to do so. Not yet. Not while Kathleen continued to come. He anticipated every visit with restless joy. Her very presence in the house filled it with sunshine and—

Perhaps only his heart felt the vibrations of happiness.

Perhaps if she, for some reason, stopped coming he would be able to leave.

But she seemed committed to regular visits. According to Rosie, she hadn't come every day until recently. Actually, what Rosie said was she hadn't come every day until Buck showed up. She'd said it with a mixture of teasing and annoyance.

"You can't stay. Have you forgotten?"

"You make sure I don't forget."

"If things were different, I would welcome you. You know it."

He nodded. "Things will never be different."

"I know, but I hope my kids can be free of our fear."

His staying put her hope at risk. He should be on his way, but still he stayed. Always giving himself one more day. Promising tomorrow he would tell Kathleen he had to leave. Then finding some excuse not to inform her, thus giving him a reason to linger one more day.

"You'll go to the Thanksgiving service with her, won't you?"

Rosie hesitated. "I'm thinking about it."

"It's your chance to leave the past behind."

"I know. To be honest, Kathleen makes me want to be closer to God."

"Me, too."

A knock informed them Kathleen had arrived. Rosie nodded at him to answer the door. "I've got Lilly." They both knew it was not the reason.

Buck's growing affection for Kathleen would only make it harder to leave. His heart wanted to see her and enjoy her company one more day. One more day to fill his insides to brimming with her sweet presence.

But one more day would never be enough.

Gritting his teeth, he pushed away the temptation to ignore the reality of his life and stay. Let people find out about his pa. Let them do what they wanted. It would be worth it to enjoy day after day of seeing Kathleen…Kathleen with the rich and powerful father.

What was he thinking? Her father had the power to destroy not only his life but also Rosie's and the children's. He had the power to make Kathleen's life miserable.

Buck vowed he'd leave before he'd allow that to happen.

He opened the door and smiled a welcome that echoed in Kathleen's eyes. Could it be she was growing fond of him, too? She'd been outspoken in her admiration, which he found endearing.

Growing fondness on her part put her future at risk, too. Her mere association with him and Rosie could destroy her. He had no wish to hurt her. For her sake he must leave soon.

Just one more day. Even better—a special outing. The idea was perfect.

He lifted her coat from her shoulders and hung it beside his own. Perhaps some of her sweet flower scent would cling permanently to his jacket, and he could think of her every time he donned it. Not that he would need such a reminder. He would carry her in his heart.

"This is wonderful weather for November," he said, setting up the discussion for his intended suggestion. Snow had fallen a week or two ago and the temperature had been cold enough to freeze the ground, but otherwise it was pleasant enough for the time of year.

"Don't be fooled into complacency," Rosie warned. "Things could change any day now."

"All the more reason to take advantage of it while we can."

Kathleen and Rosie both stared at him and the little boys clustered around his knees, but Rosie was the one to demand an explanation. "What did you have in mind?"

"A picnic."

Rosie snorted. "It might only be November but it feels a lot like winter to my way of thinking."

"Why not?" He silently appealed to Kathleen, who showed a flicker of interest. "I could rent a wagon and we could go to a pond. The kids could play on the ice and we could have a big fire. Then enjoy cocoa and sandwiches. How does that sound?" He directed his question to the kids, knowing they would show more enthusiasm than the women.

"Fun," Junior said.

"Fun," Mattie echoed.

"Sure." Joey was more guarded. Perhaps because he'd spent his share of time out in the elements.

Buck turned to Rosie first. "What do you think?"

"So long as it's not cold."

He turned to Kathleen. "You in?"

Her eyes gleamed. "I'm invited?"

"Of course." It was the reason for his idea. "Tomorrow?"

Rosie looked at the little ones. "I could feed them an early lunch so they can have their naps. That way we can enjoy the warmest part of the day."

"Then it's a plan." Buck scrubbed his hands together. One more special memory to take with him when he left.

One more excuse for delaying his departure.

The children were excited about the planned picnic, so Rosie took longer than normal to get them settled for their naps. Buck held Joey and wondered if he would have the same difficulty, but Joey soon nodded off. Buck held him even after Kathleen whispered that he had fallen asleep. He found comfort in the small body curled against him. At least he would have this bit of human contact when he left. The idea provided only a little comfort. Having met Kathleen, he now knew it would never be enough to have Joey, though he loved the boy beyond measure.

After a few minutes, he carried Joey into the bedroom. When he returned, he pulled out a bit of wood he had begun carving.

"What are you making?" Kathleen asked.

"A little horse for Joey. Watching him enjoy the toys Rosie's children have made me realize how few things Joey has. I intend to remedy it."

Her hands grew still. "You're a good father. Are there other things Joey needs that you might have overlooked, do you suppose?"

She didn't need to spell it out. He knew what she meant—the boy needed a permanent home. He agreed. But it didn't change the facts of his life—

namely that people weren't prepared to let him enjoy such luxury.

He felt her watching him. Tried to ignore it but his resistance proved fragile. He lifted his head and let her search his thoughts. Yes, Joey needed a real home. So did Buck. In his deepest, most secret dreams, he longed for the acceptance she hinted he deserved.

He knew it was a fleeting mirage.

"Joey and I will survive the best way we know how."

Slowly her expression changed, softening. "I think you are close to wanting to belong."

"Wanting to belong has never been in question." He closed his mouth firmly. He yearned to tell her everything but he dare not. It would surely put an end to her friendship. Not only with himself but also with Rosie, and Rosie didn't deserve to be robbed of Kathleen's acceptance. He pulled his gaze away and concentrated on the horse he shaped. "I think Joey will enjoy this toy."

"I'm sure he will." She didn't say anything for a spell. "Can I bring the hot cocoa for tomorrow?"

"If you like."

Rosie joined them. "I'll make sandwiches. You know, Buck, this is a good idea. I'm looking forward to an outing."

So was Buck, but for entirely different reasons that were selfish and likely dangerous. He should be leaving, not making plans to stay yet another day. Such plans were foolish and fraught with danger.

But for a little while, a precious interruption to his normal life, Buck was going to ignore the warnings of his gut.

Chapter Five

Buck loaded the children in the back of the wagon he'd rented from the livery. Rosie chose to sit in the back with the children. She slanted him a teasing smile as she got comfortable. "I'll let Kathleen sit up front with you." Her teasing vanished into warning. They both knew this interlude must end soon. Before their secret was discovered.

But for now, Buck was happy to ignore the dangers. He helped Kathleen up to the seat and took his place beside her. "Couldn't ask for better weather, could we?"

"It's beautiful."

The sun shone with golden intensity. No breeze stirred the air. Temperatures hovered at the freezing mark. Perfect for ice skating. Perfect for bonfires and winter picnics.

"Sam at the livery barn told me about a pond where people go skating. Said it was a great place for a picnic." Buck laughed. "He said he could name half a dozen couples who began their courting at a skating party there."

Kathleen laughed softly. "I know the place and two such couples. Of course, they went after dark, so maybe that makes a difference."

"'Spect so." Though he didn't intend to waste any opportunity the afternoon might present. Of course, he didn't have courting and marriage on his mind. He concentrated on guiding the wagon through a gate and down a trail toward a grove of trees. To be perfectly honest, he admitted he might have been considering both if his circumstances were different.

They weren't. But he didn't intend to let that fact rob him of one ounce of enjoyment this afternoon.

The trail led directly to a large opening. Evidence of previous fires blackened the ground. Crude wooden benches circled the burnt area. Soldierlike, bare-branched trees guarded the spot. An ice-covered pond had been partially cleared, as if used just the night before.

"This is perfect." He jumped from the wagon and assisted Kathleen to the ground. If his hands lingered at her waist longer than necessary, no one seemed to notice. He allowed himself the luxury of breathing in her scent, enjoying the reflection of the sky in her eyes, feeling the warmth of the sun from her smile before he stepped away to help Rosie and the children.

The boys squealed in delight and headed for the ice. Mattie could hardly keep his feet under him, but the other two were soon running and sliding, laughing in complete abandonment of joy. Rosie stood to the side watching, Lilly in her arms. The little girl chortled at the boys and Rosie smiled.

Kathleen moved to Buck's side. "This idea of yours is wonderful."

He grinned down at her. "I have them once in a while."

"Have what?" She managed to look confused.

"Good ideas."

Her musical laughter rang through the trees. "I'd say you have them quite often."

He let himself enjoy her praise, let himself hold her gaze while her warm look filled his heart. If only the afternoon could last forever. But he'd waste none of it.

With wood he'd brought with him and kindling gathered from the trees, he built a fire then carried the lunch basket and a knapsack to one of the benches. Kathleen followed with a jug of cocoa.

He'd brought a scoop shovel and headed for the pond. "Who wants a ride?"

The three boys scrambled to his side, slipping and sliding. "Youngest to oldest." Mattie sat on the scoop and Buck pushed him about the ice.

An hour later he was ready for a break. They trooped toward the fire, where Kathleen poured cocoa into mugs for each of them. Rosie handed out sandwiches and cookies.

He sat next to Kathleen, Joey on his other side, and Buck thought life couldn't get any better than this. A son he loved, a woman he—

He stuffed half a cookie in his mouth. Better to stick to what was possible.

"I used to come here with some friends when I was much younger." Kathleen's voice carried notes of regret and sadness.

Wishing to erase those notes, Buck shifted to study her. "Why did you stop coming?"

Her eyes filled with surprise. "You know, I can't say. Part of the reason, I suppose, is the neighbors who took me with them moved away, and I felt conspicuously alone when I came on my own. Then I got involved in other things."

The children finished their lunch and went back to play. Rosie followed them, leaving Buck and Kathleen alone. There were so many things he wanted to know about her. What she'd been like as a girl. The dreams she'd had. Which ones remained. "Tell me what types of things you're involved in."

"Up until this past fall, I spent three years attending a girls' boarding school, where we were strictly supervised. My father would expect nothing else. Of course there were those who found ways to disobey the rules." She shrugged. "I never felt the need. I loved my studies. I took on some extra projects." Her eyes glistened with pleasure at the memory. "One of the teachers led us on a study of the life of Christ. She urged us to see Him at work in this world and base our lives on how He would live."

"You really liked that, didn't you?"

"It was exactly what I needed to find purpose in my life."

"So you became a do-gooder?" Was that her only reason for befriending Rosie?

Her expression flattened. He wished he could bite back the words and bring the joy into her face again.

"I hope not. I wanted to live my life with purpose and meaning, not selfishly or with judgment. I want my life to reflect my gratitude for all God has given each of us."

He touched her hands as they lay still and peaceful in her lap. "Forgive me for speaking so harshly. From our first meeting, you have made me aware of my need to open myself up to God. Both Rosie and I were raised to love Him, but over the years I've neglected my faith."

Her eyes shone with happiness and she turned her hands into his. He twined his fingers through hers.

"Nothing would make me happier than to know you've returned to your faith." Her soft words felt like a benediction.

"Why is that?" If only he could allow himself to think it was because she cared about him in a personal way. But why was he even contemplating such a joy? He blocked from his mind the way he pictured her looking if she found out the truth about him.

Enough. He would not allow anything to mar this afternoon.

Rosie returned, Mattie at her side. "Play here with Lilly." She shifted her attention to Buck. "The bigger boys are too fast for him. They're having a great time out there."

Further conversation between himself and Kathleen was impossible. Except he had a plan. He spoke to Rosie. "Would you mind watching Joey while Kathleen and I go for a skate?"

"But I didn't bring skates." Kathleen looked so disappointed, he could have kissed her.

"I've taken care of it. Sam lent me some. Says he always keeps a few on hand." He retrieved the rucksack from the bench and pulled out two pairs of skates. "I brought some extra socks in case you needed them."

"Those look like mine," Rosie protested.

"I didn't think you'd mind."

"I don't, but it wouldn't hurt to ask."

He grinned at her. "This way I didn't have to endure any advice." Or teasing. Or warnings.

She waved away his remark. "Enjoy yourself while you can."

"I intend to." Her unspoken warning filled him with even more determination to make the most of the day. "Let me." He knelt before Kathleen, unbuckled her boots and slipped one foot at a time into the skates. He forced himself to act as if it were no different from helping Joey put on a pair of boots, but his chest muscles grew taut, making breathing difficult. Her foot was so small. So dainty. It made him want to protect her. But he was probably the worst threat she'd ever had in her life. He tightened the laces, then sat beside her to do his own. "I warn you, I haven't been on skates in a couple years."

"I haven't been since last winter."

"I suppose you skate like a dancer."

She laughed softly. "I've had lessons, if that's what you mean."

"Wonderful. You'll make me look like a clod."

She rose and held out a hand to him. "Who's watching?"

"I will be," Rosie said. "And I won't hesitate to laugh when my brother lands on his bottom."

Buck didn't give her the satisfaction of acknowledging her teasing. Instead he took Kathleen's hand and led her to the ice.

Joey saw him and slid over. "You going skating?"

"With Kathleen. You stay here with Aunt Rosie. Okay?"

Joey studied him unblinkingly for a moment, then shifted his study to Kathleen. Buck hoped he wouldn't say something to make her uneasy. But he smiled. "Okay."

Buck reached for Kathleen's hands, holding them so their arms crisscrossed in the usual skating pose. She fit perfectly at his side and matched her strides to his. He hadn't skated in a while, but discovered he had no trouble keeping on his feet. They circled the cleared area several times. She laughed as he stumbled on a corner. He held her steady when she caught her skate on a lump in the ice. A path had been cleared around the perimeter of the pond. He indicated it. "Shall we?"

"I'd love to."

They skated away from the noise, the fire and into a world where they were alone in the silence. He shifted to hold her hands and skated backward so he could watch her face. "Are you planning to return to your college in the near future?"

"I have no definite plans. Mother seems better some days, but then she gets worse again."

"What's wrong with her?"

"The doctor calls it general malaise. I know she's worse if anything upsets her, so I do my best to keep things calm in the house."

He liked the way she grew thoughtful, full of genuine concern for her mother. "You are a good daughter."

"Thank you. I try. After all, I'm their only child."

"That sounds like a huge responsibility."

She smiled gently.

Oh, how he'd grown to love her smile. If only he could capture it in his palms, tuck it in his pocket and carry it with him into the future. Then whenever he was discouraged or lonely, he could pull it out and enjoy the memory of this day.

Unfortunately he knew the memories, although all he'd have, would never suffice.

"It doesn't feel like a responsibility when it's done out of love."

He understood she would never choose someone or something over loyalty to her parents. Although he admired the trait in her, it left him feeling lonely. He forgot to move his feet. One skate caught on the ice. He churned his legs trying to keep his balance. The moment he knew it was futile, he pulled Kathleen to his chest to protect her. His feet went up. His back went down and he landed with a thud that shook the air from him. His lungs hurt. He couldn't make them work.

Kathleen lay across his chest. She pushed back to look into his face, her eyes dark blue and full of things he dared not acknowledge.

She saw he couldn't breathe and scrambled to her knees. "Buck, take a breath." She shook him a little. "Come on. You're scaring me."

His lungs decided to work, and he sucked in air until he wondered how much he could hold. He let it out in a gusty exhalation and lay there.

"Are you okay?"

He hadn't intended to frighten her, but oh, it felt good to know she would worry so about him. He sat up and grinned at her. "I'm fine, sweet Kathleen. Just fine." He got to his feet, pulling her up with him.

Sweet Kathleen, he'd called her, the sound of her name on his lips pleasant as honey. He stood facing her, studying her.

"You aren't hurt, are you?"

"I'm fine." She struggled to bring her thoughts into order. "You took the brunt of the fall."

"Let me check you over." He turned her about, brushed snow from between her shoulders, then brought her back to face him. He took his time examining her face. The warmth of his gaze on her lips brought a toe-to-hairline blush to her skin.

"There's snow stuck to your hair." He brushed it away with his fingers. They seared across her cheek.

She caught her breath as something wrenched

inside her—a sweet, fierce sensation of pleasure and hope. Her growing fondness and admiration for Buck bordered on something more profound. A feeling so new and powerful she didn't want to examine it too closely for fear it would abandon her.

"Kathleen." His husky whisper reached into her head, making it impossible to think beyond this moment when time ceased to exist.

His gaze grew more intense as he looked so deeply into her eyes, she felt his gaze touch her innermost secrets. "Kathleen," he breathed her name again, his attention on her mouth.

He lowered his head. She knew he meant to kiss her. He paused—whether to give her time to demure or to reconsider his intention, she couldn't say.

She had no desire to refuse him and tilted her head upward. His lips claimed hers, warm, firm, gentle… almost reverent. She clutched at his upper arms, holding on as the world fell away and there was nothing but them.

He ended the kiss but pulled her to his chest and pressed her face to the spot where Joey found such comfort and welcome, and she found the same. This man was a rock. An anchor. She could trust her very being to him.

"Kathleen, you are a special woman."

She smiled into the soft warmth of his coat. "Buck, you are a special man. A noble and good man."

His chuckle rumbled beneath her ear. "I love to hear you say so."

Love? Could this be love? This wonderful, satisfying, exhilarating sensation of wanting time to stop, everyone else to disappear, her life to begin at this moment? If so, she couldn't imagine anything better in the whole world.

Buck eased her back, took her hands and pressed them tight to his chest. "We need to get back."

"Of course." She'd forgotten the others. Forgotten everything but Buck. But he would never forget Joey. "I wish—"

"Shh." He pulled her closer. "Let's take what God offers us without demanding more."

It sounded like a warning not to expect anything beyond the moment. "Buck, won't you consider staying? Give people a chance to see how good and noble you are?"

He stiffened, tried to hide it. Sighed almost imperceptibly. She knew he didn't intend for her to notice. "Kathleen, I wish I could."

"Is it because of Joey?" She wanted desperately for him to say it was the reason, even though it wouldn't explain why he'd promised Rosie he would stay away even when she didn't know he had a son. "Because you need to give people a chance to accept him."

"Do you think they ever would?"

"Perhaps not everyone, but there are those who would learn to love him for his sake. I'm sure of it." Her voice rang with determination and a bunch of things she couldn't hide—longing for him to stay, a promise to stand at his side on Joey's behalf and so much more.

"I wish I could believe you, but—"

She pulled at his arms, forcing him to face her. "You can. Stay. Give people a chance to accept him. And you." No doubt her eyes revealed everything she felt, but she didn't care. She wanted him to stay. For Joey's sake, of course. For his, too. But mostly for her. She wanted a chance for this fledgling feeling of love to grow and mature. *Please, God, let him see we can have something worth staying for.*

His eyes darkened with pleasure. His grasp on her hands tightened, and his smile flooded with what she hoped was love, or at least affection. Then without warning his expression flattened, grew hard. "You make me want to stay, but believe me, there are reasons I cannot." He pulled her to his side and they continued to skate toward the bonfire.

Why? The question clung to the tip of her tongue. She stared straight ahead, seeing nothing but a shiny blur. Why couldn't he stay? Or at least tell her his reason?

"Kathleen, I'm sorry." Neither of them broke stride in their skating rhythm. "Please believe me when I say I would stay if I could. I would stay for you."

She sniffed, finding small comfort in the hopeless words. She was almost relieved they drew near to the others and Joey shouted out a greeting and raced to their side.

"Hi, Buck. You were gone long time."

"It didn't seem long to me." He squeezed Kathleen's hands to signal his reason. Having him acknowledge he wanted to stay only deepened her pain.

She smiled and chatted as they gathered together

their belongings, threw snow over the fire to douse it and returned to the wagon. The trip back to town seemed to take longer than the trip out had, and yet was over before she could think of anything to say to convince Buck that surely the reasons for staying outweighed his reasons for leaving.

They unloaded the children and picnic remnants at Rosie's. Buck turned to Kathleen, his eyes full of regret. "I'll give you a ride home, then return the wagon."

"Fine." She bid the others goodbye. She had only a few minutes to make any sort of appeal. She barely waited for him to sit beside her on the wagon. "I had hoped you might have some regard for me. That our kiss meant something more than a man and a woman falling inadvertently into each other's arms." She made no attempt to keep the hurt from her voice.

"Kathleen, I should not have kissed you, but I don't regret doing so. I do have feelings for you. But I have no right to them."

They both faced forward, mindful they rode through a town full of windows.

"You have the same rights as anyone else. The right to make a home where you choose. We are all equal in God's eyes." She left it there. How many ways could she tell him, ask him to stay without shamelessly begging? Truth is, she would beg if she thought it would make a difference.

"Not everyone is equal in man's eyes." His tone was brittle. Suddenly he turned the wagon off the road in a direction that took them away from her home. "I have to tell you something."

He drove away from town and pulled to a halt beside some sheltering trees, sending protesting birds away. He leaned over his knees. His jaw muscles clenched and unclenched. With a deep sigh he turned.

She cried out at the despair lining his face. "What is it?"

"I wish I could stay. I've found something here with you I've wanted all my adult life, though I didn't know what it was I longed for." His expression softened as he let his gaze drift over her face.

"I've found something, too." She didn't want to lose it.

Buck rolled his head back and forth in a gesture so full of sadness and defeat that she clutched his arm. He pressed his hands over hers.

"Once you hear my story you will agree I can't stay. You won't want me to."

"Can anything be that terrible?"

He nodded.

"My father—" His gaze shifted past her.

She waited. A cold trickle snaked across her shoulders. What could possibly make him so tense?

"My father was a good man." His snort of laughter was mocking. "At one time. He worked in a mill. Liked his work until a new owner bought the place. The new man expected his employees to work unreasonable hours. He took shortcuts that were dangerous. My father—" Word by word, Buck's voice grew more and more harsh. "He was injured at the mill. Broke his leg and was laid up for months. His leg never healed right. When he tried to go back to work, the mill owner said they had no room for cripples."

"Oh, Buck. How dreadful."

He grimaced. "It gets worse." Again his gaze sought distant places where she could not follow. "My mother got ill and needed medicine that Pa couldn't afford. He begged for his job or any job. Again and again he got turned away. One night Ma was suffering so. It was awful to watch. Pa walked about, angry and cursing God and the mill owner. Then he dashed from the house." The breath Buck sucked in seemed to go on forever. "He didn't come home that night. We didn't know until morning what happened. Our pa—" Buck's words were whispered agony. "Took an axe and killed the mill owner."

"Buck." It was a mere breath of a word. "Oh, Buck." Kathleen's heart had stopped beating. Her lungs had stopped drawing in air. The horror of Buck's experience filtered through a red and purple haze of shock.

"He hanged for it. Ma died. And Rosie and I—her only thirteen, me a year younger—were run out of town."

She sobbed once. Wave after wave of shock coursed through her body.

"The first town of many we were chased from. Rosie and her children deserve a chance to be accepted here. I could ruin that for them. That's why I have to leave before anyone finds out."

His words brought an abrupt end to her anguished shock. "Why must you leave? You're a good man. Let people learn that."

He grabbed her shoulders. "Am I? Or am I my father's son? Perhaps people have a reason to be afraid of me."

She caught his face between her palms and searched his gaze until she found an entrance into his thoughts. "Sins are not inherited. You are a fine, decent man whom I am honored to know."

His hungry look showed he wanted to believe her.

"Buck, you are a good man. I know it, and I think you do, too." She smiled at his look of hope. She must convince him and she leaned closer, pressed her lips to his. Startled a reaction from him. He wrapped his arms about her and pulled her close, clinging to her kiss.

Just as quickly he withdrew, but not before she'd done her best to prove her opinion of his worth. "You're a good man, Buck."

He shook his head. "Even if I believe it…even if you do, others will not. And they can make life unbearable. Believe me."

"Maybe you've never met a Sanderson before. If my father decrees you should be accepted, do you really think anyone in town will argue?" Not that she was naive enough to think everyone agreed with her father. Only that they were careful about how they expressed their differences. Nor did she think she could convince her father to change his opinion about Buck without some very convincing arguments that she would do her best to formulate.

Buck chuckled. “I see there are advantages to having a rich, powerful father. However—”

“I’d like for you to stay. Give it some thought.” She was certain his feelings for her were growing as quickly as hers for him. God willing, it would be enough to persuade him to confront his past and put it to rest.

Buck edged the wagon forward and turned them about. “I better get you home before your father comes looking for you.”

In a few minutes they reached her house. He pulled the wagon to a stop and hurried around to help her descend.

They stood facing each other, a hundred wishes swirling through her mind and likely revealing themselves on her face. She didn’t care. She wanted a chance to love this man.

He squeezed her shoulder for but a touch, then climbed to the wagon. She grabbed the side to keep him from driving away. “Promise me you’ll think about what I said.”

His smile brimmed with hope. “I’ll think about it.”

She stared after him until he turned a corner out of sight. Then she made her way up the sidewalk to face her parents, who she guessed would have watched the proceedings out the window.

Chapter Six

Buck didn't realize how much Rosie had read into the situation, though his expression likely gave away a lot. She waited until they'd had their evening meal and the children had gone to bed.

"Okay, brother, what happened between you and Kathleen?"

He examined the nail bed of his thumb. How could he begin to explain how he felt? How much he loved Kathleen and wished things could be different? "I kissed her."

Rosie shoved her cup out of the way to lean across the table. "Have you lost your mind? Do you know who she is?"

He gave her only stubborn denial. "Of course I do. She's Kathleen Sanderson. A very sweet woman."

"She's also the daughter of the richest, most powerful man in these parts." Rosie let out a noisy gust. "He would never let his sweet daughter look twice at a nobody like you. Worse than a nobody—the son of a murderer. And—" She pressed forward again. "He would stop at nothing to discredit you in her eyes. And in the eyes of all the people around here. You know how easy that will be. Why have you let it go so far? Just when I thought I might be able to forget the past."

"No one will ever let us forget the past. But perhaps it's time to stop trying to outrun it."

Rosie bolted to her feet. "You really think you can change things? Stop and think. How many times have we tried before? Having a murderer for a father marks us. It always will." She glanced about the house. "This is one of the best places I've had. I don't want to leave." She stopped at Buck's side and grabbed his face to turn it toward her. "You are going to wreck my life for nothing."

"Not for nothing. For a chance for Joey and me to belong."

She turned away from him. "Belong somewhere else."

He didn't say somewhere else would not be the same. Kathleen wouldn't be anywhere but here. Yet she didn't need him to say the words to know what he thought, and she gave a snort of disgust. "Buck, what do I have to do to get you to leave?"

He struggled between wanting to protect Rosie and longing for the love he'd ached for for so many years, he'd grown almost comfortable with the feeling.

Now, for the first time, he'd found the answer to his loneliness. Perhaps, like Kathleen said, he needed to stay and prove he deserved it.

* * *

Kathleen smiled as she stepped into the house. Buck had kissed her. She had kissed him. If the way he kissed meant anything, it wouldn't take much to convince him to stay.

She sighed as she hung her coat. She wished she knew exactly what it would take. But it seemed to be something more than she could offer. The thought clogged her heart. Why couldn't she be enough?

She turned and came face-to-face with her father.

"I came home from work early because I was worried about your mother. I found her sitting alone in the dark. Is it too much to expect you to be here when your mother needs you?"

"I'm sorry." She hurried past him to her mother's side. "Are you ill?"

"I'm very, very weary."

Kathleen rubbed her mother's hands. "What can I do?"

"Stop going to visit that woman." Her father spoke harshly.

Kathleen bowed her head. *Oh, God. Please don't let him forbid me to go.*

He went to his chair and plopped down. "I think it's time you returned to that school I paid for you to attend. It's not like you're helping your mother a lot."

"I'm not sure I want to return."

Mother took her hand. "Maybe if you simply decide to stay home instead of going *there*." She said the word with more than a hint of bitterness.

Kathleen couldn't answer. She didn't want to go

back to the college. She couldn't promise she wouldn't visit Rosie. She hoped and prayed Buck would stay. Somehow she had to convince her father to give them a chance. If only he would meet them, she was certain he'd approve of them. But she wouldn't speak her thoughts until she'd had a chance to pray about them and form a plan. *God, help me.*

She spent the rest of the afternoon at her mother's side, reading to her, fixing her tea, locating a certain necklace she thought she'd lost. It wasn't until later in the evening when her mother had gone to bed that she finally withdrew to her own room to consider the events of the day.

But rather than focus on what her father said, and how to convince him to change his mind about Buck and Rosie, her thoughts went back to the afternoon. Buck had kissed her. A kiss loaded with a thousand unspoken promises. Or so she let herself think.

She lay on her back in bed and smiled into the darkness. Surely he'd felt something. Vowing she'd try again the next day to convince him to stay, she fell asleep with a smile on her face.

But the next morning, her mother was too ill to get out of bed.

"This is on your head," Kathleen's father said. "Bringing home dirt from there. Goodness knows what your mother is ill with, thanks to you." He scowled as he prepared to leave for work.

"Mother, I'm sorry." But she had been sick off and on before she started visiting Rosie, and Kathleen was certain she had not brought sickness home with her.

Her mother slept fitfully throughout the morning and sat up in bed for a lunch of clear soup and crackers. "I'm so weak," she murmured as she pushed away the tray without finishing.

"Can I do anything?" Kathleen refrained from glancing at the clock.

"Could you read to me? I really like the story you started the other day."

Kathleen could not refuse her mother, even though it meant she would not be able to go to Rosie's today. She got the book and settled in next to her mother to read. But it was only words she recited. Her mind was not on the story. If only she could send a message to Buck and let him know why she couldn't be there.

But she'd have to wait until tomorrow and an improvement in Mother's well-being.

At the knock at the door, Buck looked up from playing with the boys and helping Rosie. Had the morning passed so quickly? Or was Kathleen early? He knew the answer. It was much earlier than she normally arrived.

He headed for the door, eager to see her and judge if she'd changed her mind about him. He broke stride. What if she'd come to say they could no longer be friends?

He brushed his finger across his mouth. Her kiss said they could be friends and so much more.

Throughout the night, he'd considered if she could be right. Would people give him a chance to start over here if they knew the truth? Or could he expect to hide it from them? He'd mentally explored ways of disguising his true identity. A false name would be easy enough but carried no guarantees. Experience had taught him that nothing did.

He opened the door, his smile wide in greeting. A man stood before him, scowling. Buck's smile flattened in an instant.

"You would be Buck, I presume. Buck Donahue."

His heart plummeted to the soles of his feet. So much for hiding his name. "And you would be?"

"Samuel Sanderson. I'm Kathleen's father."

"I see. Would you like to step inside?" Not that he felt exactly welcoming at the way the scowling man regarded him.

"I think I prefer to remain here. What I have to say won't take long."

Buck stepped outside and pulled the door shut behind him. He was pretty sure the kids didn't need to hear whatever the man was about to say. Rosie would guess correctly what it was.

Mr. Sanderson cleared his throat and drew himself up tall. Buck saw no resemblance to his daughter. Kathleen wore a countenance of love and joy. Just looking at her made others feel special. Her father made him feel dirty, despised.

"My daughter has been spending a lot of time here. I didn't approve when it was just your sister and her children. But when I heard a brother had arrived... well, it was my duty to discover what sort of person you are." He waited, as if expecting Buck to fill in the details.

He didn't intend to supply one single fact.

"I learned who you are, Mr. Donahue. I know about your father, Michael Donahue. How dare you think you can even breathe the same air as my daughter? I suggest you leave town immediately. We have no use for the likes of you in our presence. Kathleen doesn't care to see you again." He adjusted the lapels on his coat and turned to leave. Then paused. "I expect you'll be on your way by morning."

It wasn't a suggestion. Yet Buck didn't flinch before the man's demanding glare. Kathleen didn't care to see him again? He didn't believe it.

"I won't be run out of town on your say-so." He leaned forward, his eyes burning with determination. "I will not believe Kathleen doesn't want to see me again unless I hear the words from her mouth."

He dared not contemplate hearing such words.

Mr. Sanderson grunted. "You won't see her again, I promise you that." He stomped away without a backward look.

Buck did not return immediately to the house. He knew he must first compose himself so as not to give away anything to Rosie or keen-eyed Joey. A few minutes later he shivered in the cold and stepped inside.

Joey glanced up, studied Buck closely. Before the boy asked a question, Buck got very busy cleaning up the dirty dishes. Thankfully, Rosie had taken Lilly to the bedroom.

He kept busy but the words spoken by Mr. Sanderson circled inside his head like angry hornets.

I know about your father. How dare you? You won't see her again.

But Kathleen cared about him. She would find a way to at least say goodbye.

The morning, which had gone so fast until this point, slowed down to endless ticks on the clock. He could not expect her earlier than normal, but he tried not to hold his breath, to force his heart to beat again and again until the time arrived.

Rosie came from the bedroom. "Did I hear some-one at the door?"

"I don't know. Did you?"

She rolled her eyes. "You know I did. Who was it?"

He couldn't bear to tell her. But soon enough the word would be out. "Later," he said, indicating the children clustered about the table.

Her eyes widened. "No. It can't be."

He nodded. "It is."

"I knew this would happen. I warned you, but would you listen? No. You let your heart rule your head. For what? You'll never have her. Instead you ruin my chances."

"Rosie, I'm sorry."

She drew her lips back in resignation as she looked about her small house. "It's not much, but this is my home. I don't want to move."

Joey edged closer, acutely aware of the tension in the air. "You move? Why? This nice house."

Rosie pulled him to her side. "You're right. I guess I'll stay as long as I can."

Buck rubbed his neck and wished life could be different. "Maybe once we're gone it won't matter."

Her eyes filled with sorrow. "It always matters."

"I know. I should have left long ago."

"We go?" Joey's eyes widened. "Where we go? This good place. I like it here. I like cousins. I like Aunt Rosie."

"I know you do. But this isn't home." Would he ever be able to offer his son a proper home?

Only if he stayed.

He straightened. Considered Rosie. Would staying hurt her chances of acceptance?

She watched him, her eyes narrowing. "Are you thinking what I think you are?"

"Probably."

"Then reconsider. I beg you."

"If Kathleen accepts us, don't you think the rest of the community will?"

"Buck, don't start expecting miracles."

He laughed. "Why not? Don't you believe God loves us as much as He loves the Sandersons?"

"I don't think it's God who runs the store and refuses service or who crosses the street to avoid a person."

His enthusiasm died. "You're right, of course." But Kathleen had almost convinced him it was possible to stay here and start a real life.

They ate lunch, but he barely heard a word of the children's talk as he waited for Kathleen to show up.

But it wasn't Mr. Sanderson's warning words

taking up the space in his mind. It was the assurance of her sweet smile and total acceptance.

He could barely finish his meal as his anticipation grew. As soon as the children appeared to be done, he jumped up and began to gather the dirty dishes.

Soon the dishes were washed and dried and back in the cupboard. The table had been scoured to within an inch of annihilation. He stared out the window. The weather was clear. No impending storm to keep her away.

Sighing, he turned. Rosie had gone to the bedroom with Lilly and her boys. No doubt they were all sleeping.

Joey refused to go to bed. "I want to wait for Miss Kathleen."

"Have your nap so you'll be ready to visit her when she comes."

"I'll go to bed but I won't sleep." He got the stubborn look on his face that Buck knew well.

Kathleen was late. Something must have happened to delay her. He walked to the window to look out and saw nothing but snow-dusted grass and the empty beaten path leading to the center of town.

He turned to stare at the door. Perhaps she had knocked and he hadn't heard her. In a flurry of hope and despair he crossed the room and threw open the door, only to be greeted by a blast of cold air and nothing more. Quickly, he closed the door and leaned against it.

Time crept past on heavy, dragging feet.

The children came from the bedroom, sleepy-eyed

and tousle-haired. Joey looked carefully around the room, as if expecting to find Kathleen in a corner. "She not come?"

"No. She didn't." Her father was right when he said she wouldn't come again. His insides tore open to realize she would turn her back on him because of her father's decision. But all along he'd tried to tell himself this would happen.

Rosie joined them. She gave him a look of sympathy but refrained from saying, "I told you so."

She didn't need to.

He had no more reason to stay. Only one thing would have made him change his mind, and Kathleen had not given him that invitation.

There was nothing he could do about it.

The afternoon passed on leaden feet as Kathleen read to her mother and spent time amusing her. When she finally dozed, the day was too far gone to dash over to Rosie's. Besides, she hesitated to leave her mother alone. She'd been really down all day.

She slipped from the room and hurried to kneel beside her bed. Why did God allow these delays? She wanted so much to be with Buck. Yesterday she'd felt he was very close to changing his mind about leaving. Her soul calmed as she prayed. Hearing her father enter the house, she returned to the sitting room. "Mother is sleeping. She's been restless all day."

"Good. I need to talk to you alone. Sit down."

She perched on the edge of the chair, wondering

what called for such a serious look on her father's face. *Please don't let him forbid me to go to Rosie's.*

He folded his hands in his lap and looked so stern, her nerves twitched. "It's time you heard the truth about your friends."

"You mean Rosie?"

"Yes. And her brother."

She refrained from saying she knew all she needed to know.

"I took the liberty of doing a little investigation about your friends."

"Rosie and Buck," she insisted. "They have names."

"I am deeply disturbed by what I've discovered."

She guessed what he was about to say but kept her peace, knowing he must speak the words before she could offer any defense.

"You were too young to know the details and even if you weren't, we would have shielded you from such grizzly information, but I think you must now know it all. About ten years ago there was a cold-blooded murder in a mill town in Colorado. I'll spare you the worst part, but let me simply say a man considered himself unjustly dealt with and took matters into his own hands. Revenge, plain and simple. He butchered the man who owned the mill." Father hesitated as if he knew more. "It was beastly. Needless to say, the man was hanged for murder."

She nodded. She'd heard it all from Buck, so it wasn't the shock it might have been.

"That man was named Michael Donahue. To this day, if you mention his name people get angry and upset. He killed a man with high connections and people aren't about to forget it."

Kathleen's father studied her closely. "Did you know your friends are Donahues?"

"Yes, I knew. Buck told me about it."

"You can understand why his offspring are not welcome in any community."

"But why? They had nothing to do with what happened."

"The acorn doesn't fall far from the tree." Her father shook his head as if he regretted his belief.

"Father, I respectfully disagree."

His face grew thunderous. Long ago she had learned to obey without arguing in order to avoid his disapproval, but never before had there been anything she felt so keenly she must defend.

"If you would but meet them, you would see they are both good and noble people who are living honorable lives. When has a child ever been held responsible for a parent's actions? Buck and Rosie were only twelve and thirteen at the time."

Her father rose to his feet, his posture so stiff she knew she had both offended and shocked him with her defense of the pair. "For your protection I don't intend to tell others, so long as that man leaves town."

He heart grew leaden at her father's stubbornness. "They're good people."

"You surely can't still believe that." He sat back down and leaned forward. "Kathleen, I must do what I think is best for you, as I always have. Just as I did with those other friends of yours."

"What do you mean?" She shivered, sensing she wouldn't like what he was about to say.

"You must have guessed what happened to the Rempels and why friends from your school don't contact you."

"No, Father. Tell me why." Cold dread iced her veins at what he suggested.

"I persuaded Mr. Rempel to move on to a better job. Took care of them very well. I allowed only letters from friends I considered appropriate."

"Father, how could you? You've confined me to a lonely life. And I blamed myself. I thought there was something wrong with me that made all my friends disappear." Her voice cracked and she clamped her mouth shut lest she say things she'd regret.

Her father looked confused for a moment, then his expression cleared. "I only did what I thought was best, and I always will."

"Kathleen." Her mother's voice came from her bedroom and Kathleen excused herself, grateful to have a reason to discontinue the conversation. But she might have swallowed thorns at the way her insides bled.

Chapter Seven

Kathleen tried to still her restless concern throughout the night, but she wanted nothing more than to rush to Buck's side and assure him she did not agree with her father.

But first she must spend the morning with her mother who insisted she was well enough to be up. She didn't want Kathleen to read to her. She didn't have any project she cared about doing. "I'm bored. If I felt stronger I would visit one of my friends." She sounded petulant.

"Would you like to help with a project I'm working on? It's a quilt."

Mother brightened. "I might like that."

Kathleen got the basket she'd brought from Rosie's and took out the unfinished top. "I'm helping Rosie make this for one of her children. They don't have enough warm bedding, so they'll truly appreciate it."

Her mother examined the needlework. Each square had been carefully stitched to the next with firm, even stitches that would last a good long time. "This is fine work. Did you do this?"

Kathleen looked at the section her mother examined. "Rosie did that." She moved the quilt. "I did this part."

Mother bent over the handwork. "Both of you do fine sewing."

Kathleen studied her mother. "Are you surprised I stitch a fine seam? Or that Rosie does?"

She fingered the material. "Both, I think. You were taught to do things like needlework and cross-stitch. This is so…"

"Practical?"

Mother's smile was full of self-mockery. "That makes me sound shallow."

"I don't mean to insinuate such. But there is something satisfying about knowing I'm working on a project to keep a little boy warm at night."

Mother took up a needle and thread and began to sew a square into the pattern. "Tell me about the little boy."

"It's Rosie's son, Junior. He's four years old and so grown up in some ways. Mattie, his little brother, is two, and Junior watches out for him."

"There are two children?"

"Three." She told about Lilly next. "And Rosie's brother has a child." She wondered how much to tell, but her heart overflowed. "Mother, I want to tell you about Rosie's brother. His name is Buck and he's adopted a little boy he found alone on the prairie." She repeated Joey's story.

"He's a half-breed child?"

"Yes, Mother." She prayed for wisdom to discuss this. After all, if Buck remained in the area and their relationship developed as she hoped, her mother would have to confront this issue. "That's his heritage, but who he is, what matters to people who know him, is that Joey is a very observant little boy who cares about how others feel. He's very loyal." She repeated some of the things Joey had said to defend Buck. "Buck is a loving, kind father."

Mother studied Kathleen. "This Buck—what do you know about him?"

Her fingers grew still as she met Mother's eyes. "I know all I need to know. I admire him greatly for doing what he knows is right, even though he understands some will frown at his choice to adopt Joey. He's a good man, Mother. I wish you would meet him. I think you'd like him."

The way her mother's gaze darted away told Kathleen she wasn't ready to accept Buck into her home. "Mother, I am growing very fond of him."

"Your father told me about him. His father is a murderer."

"But that isn't who he is. Don't you see? He needs people to see past what his father did to who he is."

"Kathleen, do you really think the community would ever accept him, knowing about his father? And seeing the boy he's adopted? People don't forgive and forget easily."

"I think I am growing to love Buck. I haven't told him so but I will. I don't want to be controlled by what people might say and miss God-given possibilities." There. She'd said it and it felt good and right. "I do not want to disappoint you and Father, but your caution about Rosie and Buck is misplaced and I intend to continue visiting them. If Buck returns my affections as I think he does, I will not reject him because of his father—and certainly not because of his son."

They stared at each other a long moment. Kathleen sensed no disapproval or censure in her mother's gaze. Dare she hope her mother understood the depth of Kathleen's feelings and would honor them?

She reached for one of Kathleen's hands. "I believe your motives are pure and honorable. But I fear this whole thing is out of your hands."

Kathleen jerked back. "What do you mean?"

"Your father visited this Buck—" she broke off as if the word stung her tongue "—yesterday and told him he wasn't welcome in our town."

Kathleen bolted to her feet. "Yesterday!" And she'd stayed home to care for her mother. "I must go. I must stop him from leaving."

"My dear, I expect you are too late."

"I must try." She raced for the door. If Mother forbade her—oh, she hoped it wouldn't come to that. She didn't want to be forced to disobey her mother.

But Mother watched her depart without uttering a word.

Buck stuffed the last of his belongings into the saddlebag. "I hope you will go to the Thanksgiving service. You and the kids deserve a chance to be accepted."

Rosie sat at the table watching his every move, her face a study in misery. "I don't have a lot to be thankful for. If only things could be different for both of us."

Three little boys clustered about Buck. Joey wore an expression of resignation. "We not staying ever, are we?"

The words scraped at Buck's head. He would love to give Joey a permanent home. "Don't make this any harder than it has to be, okay, little buddy?"

Joey nodded. "I go quietly."

Buck chuckled. "You make it sound like a walk to the gallows."

"What's that?"

"Never mind." He shouldn't have used that word and couldn't meet Rosie's gaze for fear she would be upset. "Joey, time to say goodbye."

Joey hugged his cousins and kissed Rosie.

Buck's heart sat heavy in his chest, weighed like ten gallons of cold water as Buck also hugged the children and kissed Rosie. "We'll walk to the livery barn and get our horses." He paused at the door. "Tell Kathleen goodbye for me if you get a chance."

Rosie nodded. "I will."

They both knew she might never get an opportunity. Kathleen may never again visit.

Joey strode at Buck's side, every step filled with determination. His loyalty to Buck meant he would always tuck in his chin and move when Buck moved.

"Buck, it's my fault, isn't it?"

"What is?"

"That we got to leave again. It's 'cause I'm Indian. I hear people say bad things about me. Call me dirty."

Buck stumbled. When had he heard such awful things? Of course, there were those who didn't consider Joey worth common courtesy. If only he could prevent such nasty talk. But he couldn't. And every time they moved on, Buck reinforced Joey's belief. "Buddy, it isn't because of you. It's because of me. Or I suppose, because of my father."

"But your father dead."

"Yes, he is." Someday he would have to tell Joey the whole truth, but not yet.

"Why a dead man tell you what to do?"

He stopped stock-still halfway across the street. Why did his father still control his life? Or Kathleen's father, for that matter? Would people ever stop telling him to move on? Seemed like too much to hope for. "Come on, Joey. We've got things to tend to."

Kathleen paused before Rosie's door and struggled to catch her breath. *Please, let me be in time to stop him.* She knocked.

Rosie answered the door, Lilly perched on her hip. She studied Kathleen from head to toe and back, then stepped aside to allow her entrance. "I didn't expect you again."

Kathleen glanced about the room. Mattie and Junior played on the floor. Her heart hammered a protest against her ribs. "Where is he?"

"He's gone." Rosie tried to sound hard but her voice trembled, gave away her sorrow.

"Gone? I'm too late?" She pressed a fist to her mouth to stifle a moan. "But he promised he would tell me before he left."

"I think all promises are off." Rose's voice tightened. "What did you expect? Your father told him to leave town. Told him you wouldn't come again. Then you didn't show up. How did you think he'd take it?"

"I wanted to come yesterday, but Mother was ill. She needed me."

"I expect she did."

Kathleen lifted her face to study Rosie. A dreadful thought formed. "You think she pretended to be sick to keep me from coming?"

Rosie shrugged. "What do you think?"

"I don't know. I suppose it's possible. Today I informed her I intended to keep visiting here." Ignoring the heat stealing up her cheeks, she continued. "I told her I care about Buck. That's when she told me Father had been here. I didn't know until then."

Rosie didn't change her expression. She wasn't convinced.

"You must believe me."

"Buck's life is hard enough without some rich girl toying with him."

Kathleen jerked back. "You think—? No. It's not like that at all."

"Really?"

"Rosie, how can you say that? I thought we were friends." She scrubbed at the tickle in her nose.

Things were not turning out at all the way she hoped. She pressed the heels of her hands to her eyes. God help her.

"I don't want to see Buck hurt anymore. He has very deep feelings."

Kathleen grabbed Rosie's hands. "I know. He is a good, honorable man. Tell me where he's gone. I love him and must find him and tell him so. If he won't stay, I'll go with him. I don't care where we go. Please tell me where I can find him."

Rosie studied her a long moment, measuring her words, no doubt, against her father's. After a bit, she sighed. "He and Joey were going to the livery barn to get their horses. You might catch them if you hurry." She sounded doubtful, but Kathleen didn't pay any heed.

"I'll find him. I will. If he's gone I'll hire someone to ride after him." She dashed out the door and raced across town to the livery barn. Upon arrival, she glanced about the yard, didn't know if to be relieved or disappointed when she saw no one in the pen outside the barn. She stepped inside, giving her eyes a moment to adjust to the dim interior.

The livery man watched her. She gasped in air so she could speak. "I'm looking for a man and a boy. Have you seen them?"

"Would it be a particular man and boy or will any do?"

She laughed a little at the unexpected humor. "A tall, good-looking man and a dark-haired little boy."

He removed his hat and scratched his haystack hair. "Half-breed maybe?"

"The boy is." She waited in an agony of uncertainty as the man considered her answer.

"Uh-huh."

"You've seen them?"

He nodded past her. "Could that be them?"

She turned, saw Buck standing in the shadows grinning at her and sprang toward him. "Buck, you haven't left."

"So I'm a tall, good-looking man? I like that."

She ground to a stop, embarrassment racing up her neck and pooling in her cheeks. "Rosie said you were leaving," she whispered.

He bent to Joey. "Son, go play with the cat you found in the back."

Joey looked from one to the other as if seeking reassurance. "You not going to change your mind?"

"She said I was good-looking."

Joey grinned and dashed off.

Buck resumed his casual stance, one booted foot resting on the toe. Sure didn't seem in a hurry to leave. "Why are you here?"

There wasn't time to play silly games. He had to know what she felt. "To stop you from leaving."

"Why?"

"I think you know the answer."

He pushed his Stetson back, and the light from the door made his eyes look intense. "You didn't come yesterday."

"Mother was ill and I couldn't leave her."

He acknowledged her explanation with a slight tilt of his head. "Your father paid me a visit."

"I know. Please don't think he speaks for me."

He waited, studying her.

She wanted…expected…more—a welcome. A hug at the least. Then she realized what he needed. "Buck, you are a good and noble man. I cannot imagine how difficult life has been for you." Her words were coming out in a jumble. She hoped he could arrange them into a meaningful order. "All these years you have been driven away by people's opinion, but if you stay here I promise you I will stand at your side no matter what people say."

"What about your father?"

She hoped her mother had softened toward the Donahues. Maybe Father would, too. If not, she would do her best to bridge the gap between them. "I will not let him decide who I befriend. What better place to start over than right here where there are already people who accept you?"

"Friends, is it?"

She grinned. "I never said that was all." She took a step closer. "Buck, I think I love you."

"Kathleen, I know I love you." He pulled her into his arms and held her close, his cheek pressed to her head. He eased back, caught her chin in his fingers and lifted her face toward him. Slowly, his eyes adoring her as he lowered his head, he claimed her lips in a kiss so full of love and promise that a sob stalled in her chest.

The kiss ended and she sighed. "You're going to stay then?"

"I am indeed. I've got a job here at the livery barn for the winter. After that, well, we'll see."

"You'd already decided to stay before I begged you to."

He chuckled. "I decided Joey deserves a chance to know family and home and to be accepted. I figured it was time I gave myself the same chance."

A rustle to the side drew their attention to a little boy watching with a guarded expression. "You taking Buck?"

Kathleen held out a hand toward the boy. "I'm taking you both."

Grinning so hard his eyes flashed, he threw his arms around both of them. "I take you, too."

Buck scooped him into his arms and kissed Joey on one cheek while Kathleen kissed him on the other.

She reached for Buck's hand. "People can be so unfair."

"But others can be so kind. Like you."

After Joey returned to playing with the cat, Kathleen leaned over and kissed Buck. They might face those who would judge Buck or Joey unfairly, but they would stand together and enjoy the good people in life.

A few hours later she prepared to return home. "I volunteered to decorate the church for Thanksgiving tomorrow. Will you help me?"

"Are you sure I should?"

"Very sure."

He kissed her. "I'll be there."

She hurried away to face her parents. She did not look forward to informing them Buck was staying in town and she intended to be his friend and more, but she faced them with determination and gave her little speech. "All I can say is this—Buck is a good man and I am honored to know him. I want your approval, but if you refuse it I must follow my heart." Father looked shocked and she hurried from the room before he could speak.

The next afternoon she met Buck at the church and they arranged the bounty people had brought in all morning—sheaves of grain, huge orange pumpkins, baskets of potatoes, branches of red leaves, jars of beans and beet pickles. "There is so much," she murmured as they stood side by side admiring the rich display.

"This bounty is nothing compared to what's in here." Buck pressed his palm to his chest. "My heart is full to overflowing. First, that a woman like you could love a man like me." His eyes filled with wonder. "Secondly, that I have found a place where I belong."

"You belong right here." She pressed her own palm to her chest. "Where my heart overflows with love and gratitude."

"Gratitude?"

"Yes, for a man such as you to love. And that you didn't leave." She'd told him how her father had sent so many of her friends away without her knowledge.

"I discovered it's hard to walk away from a pretty

woman." He pulled her into his arms. "Even harder to walk away from love."

She raised her face. "Isn't it amazing that we discover our love at Thanksgiving?"

"It's really a season of bounty," he murmured before he claimed her lips.

As she prepared for the service that night, she prayed Buck and Rosie would be welcomed as she believed they should be.

She walked with her parents toward the church, thankful they did not take her to task about her decision. The evening was pleasantly warm, unstirred by a breeze. Stars glistened overhead. At the church the milling crowd hummed with anticipation. It had been a bountiful year and people were grateful.

As they drew closer, Kathleen noticed a little boy who looked up at the stained-glass window and said, "He's smiling at me."

Kathleen sniffled as she saw that the child looked into the face of Jesus. She signaled to her parents. "It's Joey, Buck's boy." She glanced about, located Buck standing next to Rosie across the yard. She pointed him out to her parents. "I'm going to welcome them." Without giving either of them a chance to suggest otherwise, she made her way through the crowd to Buck's side and reached for his hand. She greeted Rosie.

Buck smiled and squeezed Kathleen's hand. "Joey is fascinated by the stained-glass window."

"He sees the love of Jesus."

Kathleen felt a nudge at her elbow and turned. "Mother?"

"Would you introduce your friends?"

Bursting with joy at this welcome, Kathleen did so. She looked about for Father. When he saw her silent invitation, he stalked across and allowed himself to be introduced before he backed away. It was a start. After that, several others welcomed the newcomers.

"Thank you," she whispered to her mother.

"You made me realize if I thought more of others and their needs, I'd have less time to dwell on my aches and pains."

Kathleen wrapped her arm around Buck's and they joined the movement toward the door. Tomorrow everyone would sit down with family and celebrate their gratitude. Kathleen would enjoy dinner with her family. Then she'd join Rosie and Buck and their children for another bountiful feast.

Tonight they shared their hearts of thanks with their church family. She sat at his side and sang hymns of Thanksgiving with more joy than she'd ever before known.

And the way Buck smiled down at her, she knew he shared her gratitude.

Epilogue

Kathleen checked the table set for eight. The best china and crystal shone. She wanted these guests to be treated with every honor they'd have bestowed on any of her father's business associates. She turned to her mother. "I'm so grateful that you invited Rosie and Buck and their children for Thanksgiving dinner." This morning her mother announced that Cook had been instructed to prepare more than originally planned, and she'd sent a messenger to Rosie's house to ask them to share the meal with them. Kathleen had hugged her mother with joy and anticipation.

"It seems we are about to be closely associated with them. Besides, I do believe it will be fun to have children at the table for a change."

Kathleen refrained from saying it would be a welcome change for her. Not only the children, but also to have people she cared about sharing the day. "You're sure Father is okay with this?"

Her mother's smile seemed a trifle uncertain. "No

matter how your father feels, you can count on him to conduct himself in a hospitable way."

"That's true." She glanced at the mantel clock. Dinner would soon be ready. Suddenly overcome with nervous energy, she hurried to look out the window. Would Buck be comfortable in these formal surroundings? Would he win the approval of her father? Then she sucked in a calming breath. Her father might know how to conduct himself in an acceptable fashion, but so did Buck. More than that, Buck had learned to meet slighting glances without flinching. She prayed it wouldn't come to that. "Here they are." She left the window, then returned. "There's another man with them. Who could it be?" He held baby Lilly in one arm. Rosie clung to his other side. "It must be Rosie's husband. Quick, put out another place." As her mother did so, Kathleen rushed to the door. But her father was there ahead of her.

"I'm the host. I'll invite them in."

So Kathleen waited as her father opened the door. Buck stepped forward and offered his hand. Kathleen's father took it without hesitation. Then Buck introduced the man at Rosie's side. "Her husband, Bill."

"I hope you don't mind that he's come along unexpectedly," Rosie said.

"Not at all," Kathleen assured her.

Bill shook hands with her father. "The boss gave us all a few days off and said to go visit our families. Last chance to get out before Christmas. I jumped at the offer." The way he smiled at Rosie and the children said better than words how much he'd missed them.

Rosie stole a furtive look around the hallway and peeked into the front room. "So this is your house."

"Want a tour?"

"Oh, I couldn't." Then she grinned. "But I'd love to."

"Come along, then. All of you." She led them down the hall. "Father, you, too. After all, it's your house."

Her mother joined them, too, and they traipsed from one room to the next.

Rosie's eyes grew more and more round, but Buck's expression seemed tight. Kathleen edged up to him. "What's wrong?" They dropped back so the others wouldn't hear them.

"I can never compete with this. All I can offer you is a simple home, probably a lot like Rosie's."

She pressed a hand to his cheek. "You can offer me more than that."

He shook his head, not understanding.

"You can offer me your warm love. It's better than anything these rooms can give me."

The tension fled from his eyes. "That I can certainly do."

The others had disappeared into yet another room. Buck took her hands between his and held them to his heart. "Kathleen, I love you more than words can tell. I want to spend the rest of my life with you making you happy, sharing both our joys and our sorrows. Will you marry me?"

Her heart thrilled within her. She'd been a tiny

bit worried he might want to hold off asking her this question. But she had no doubts. No hesitation. "I will gladly marry you." They kissed quickly as they heard the others returning. But his eyes promised more later.

Joey rushed to them. "Buck, they got all sorts of rooms but nobody to live in them. Just empty rooms for things." Then his voice saddened. "Grown-up things. No toys."

Kathleen glanced at her father, wondering what he thought of this assessment of his fine house. He drew back as if the words had hit him in an unfamiliar spot. Then he blinked and relaxed visibly.

"I suppose we are sadly lacking in things for children. Perhaps, young man, you'd like to come shopping with me this week and help me choose things to remedy the situation."

"You really mean it?"

Father nodded. "I never say things I don't mean."

"I'd like to do that," Joey said, "if it's okay with Buck."

Buck readily agreed.

Kathleen sidled up to her father. "Thank you."

He squeezed her shoulder but said nothing.

"Dinner is served," her mother called, and they filed into the dining room. A golden roasted turkey sat before her father's place, stuffing spilling from its cavity. Other bowls held heaps of mashed potatoes and a variety of vegetables. The white tablecloth provided a perfect backdrop for the china, crystal and silver. Sunlight streamed from the window and hit the china cupboard, sending shards of rainbow light across the table.

"Oh," Rosie gasped. "It's beautiful." And it truly was.

"Thank you." Kathleen's mother sounded pleased. She indicated where each should sit.

Kathleen and Buck sat on one side of the table with Joey at Buck's side. Buck took her hand under the table and squeezed it.

Her father glanced around the table. "I wish to welcome all of you today. We are honored to have you in our home. Traditionally at this time of year, we share what we're thankful for. I'd like to begin." He turned to Kathleen. "I'm proud and pleased to have a daughter who is bold enough to stand up for her own beliefs. Even against her father."

Kathleen blinked back tears and Buck chuckled, his grip growing firmer.

Bill spoke next. "I am grateful for a job and for a wife and kids to love." His voice choked at the end and Rosie's eyes glistened with tears.

"I am blessed to have a friend like Kathleen," Rosie said, and Kathleen sniffled even as she smiled.

The little boys spoke. Junior said he was glad to have a cousin to play with and Mattie, stumbling over the words, said he liked having a mama and papa. Lilly, too young to speak, sat on her mother's knee and grinned.

Kathleen looked to her mother at the end of the table, wondering if her parent would realize how much she had to be thankful for.

Her mother cleared her throat before she began. "A few days ago I considered myself a lonely, useless woman, but thanks to my daughter—" she reached for Kathleen's hand "—I realize that my vision was too narrow." She indicated the room. "I have so much—a fine husband and a generous daughter. Plus the means to help others, and with my husband's blessing I intend to do more of that in the future."

Kathleen's heart clogged with emotion. "Mother, you make me so proud."

Then it was Kathleen's turn. She could barely speak for the emotions overwhelming her. "I don't know where to begin. I'm grateful for my parents. For my upbringing. I'm grateful for my new friends—"

"You mean me, too?" Joey asked, his voice anxious.

"I mean you and Buck. I love you both very much."

Joey nodded his pleasure and only then did Kathleen let herself meet Buck's eyes. His gaze burned with love and gratitude and a whole lot more that she hoped he'd tell her once they were alone.

Her father tapped the table to bring their attention back to the others. "Buck, what are you thankful for?"

Buck chuckled. "I expect everyone here already knows. It's Kathleen. Her love has set my heart free. Sir." He faced her father. "She has agreed to marry me. Do we have your blessing?"

Kathleen drew in a sharp breath and held it. This was a lot for her father to take in at once. He studied Kathleen for a moment. She could see that he struggled with his desire to have her marry well, in a way that would perhaps improve his position in the eyes of others. "Father, I love him."

He nodded. "Then you have my blessing."

"Thank you."

Buck echoed the thanks.

"And you, young man." Her father turned to Joey. "What are you thankful for?"

Kathleen could see that despite any initial reservations he had, her father was charmed by Joey's directness and keen observation.

Joey flashed a grin to everyone. "I glad for everything and everyone." His eyes settled on the waiting food. "Mostly I very glad we don't have to eat rabbit."

The adults laughed at his comment.

"I think we better eat." Kathleen's father prayed and then began to carve the turkey. Food was passed, and everyone relaxed and visited like old friends.

Kathleen glanced about the table. Never before had she enjoyed such a Thanksgiving feast in this place. "I am so blessed," she murmured, not caring if anyone heard.

But Buck, attuned to her as he was, leaned close. "God's bounty overflows to us."

She held his gaze a moment, forgetting everyone else. Life with this man would be a continual sharing of God's love. "I love you," she whispered.

"And I love you," he whispered back.

What greater bounty could either of them ask for than this precious shared love?

* * * * *

Dear Reader,

I loved Thanksgiving Day when I was a child. It meant a trip to a small country church where special services were held—an annual tradition. A two- or three-hour service took up the afternoon. In this service the local men got up one after another and spoke for ten or fifteen minutes, telling us what they were thankful for. Then we had a break that allowed the children to go outdoors and run about in the dusty grass of fall while the meal was set out. Turkey, all the fixings, mounds of mashed potatoes, vegetables and salads and then a stunning array of pies. Mmm-mmm good. Another, shorter service was held in the evening. I loved the socializing. I loved the food. I loved hearing what people were thankful for. So when I was asked to write a Thanksgiving novella, I jumped at the chance. I hope you catch a bit of the thankfulness my characters felt. And may each of us learn to be more thankful.

I love to hear from readers. Contact me through email at linda@lindaford.org. Feel free to check on updates and bits about my research at my website, www.lindaford.org.

God bless,

Linda Ford

Questions for Discussion

1. Kathleen has had a privileged upbringing. How has it affected her? Is she thankful for what she's been blessed with? Is there a downside to her privilege?

2. Buck's young life was shattered by a tragic event. How did you feel about what happened to him? Would it have colored your feelings toward him if you lived then?

3. What things did Kathleen see in Buck that made her admire him? What do they say about him?

4. Why do you think Kathleen wanted to befriend Rosie? What led her to this desire? What can you learn from her choices and actions?

5. Do you think Buck and Kathleen will have an easy life? Why or why not? And how do you think they will handle challenges? What part can thankfulness have in their future?

6. What lessons did Kathleen's parents need to learn? Do you think they did? Is there any evidence of it in the story?

HOME FOR THANKSGIVING

Winnie Griggs

To my wonderful family—husband, children, mother, siblings—who have been enthusiastic supporters and all-around cheerleaders for me through the ups and downs of my writing career.

The Lord upholds all those who fall
and lifts up all who are bowed down.
—*Psalms* 145:14

Chapter One

November 1894
Cleebit Springs, Texas

It was now or never.

Ruby Tuggle had been sitting in the hotel lobby when Mr. Lassiter returned from whatever business he'd been conducting. She'd watched him climb the stairs to his room, looking as though he'd had a rough day, and then come back down thirty minutes later, cleaner but still tired-looking.

From her seat in the secluded corner of the lobby she'd had a clear view into the hotel dining room. Watching his profile as he ate his meal, she'd tried to get some sense of the man himself.

She'd memorized the way his dark hair tried to curl around his ears, the way it just barely touched his collar in the back and the slight impression of where his hat had rested. She'd watched the way he politely interacted with Mrs. Dowd when she'd brought out his food, and how he'd kept to himself otherwise.

And the more she studied him, the more solid her gut feeling grew. No doubt about it, he was a good man, and God had put him in her path to help her.

Just now he'd set his cutlery down, sat back and reached for his glass, a sure sign that he was nearly finished with his meal. Soon he would get up and return to his room. If she didn't gather her courage to speak to him now, she likely wouldn't get another chance.

Taking a deep breath, Ruby rose and moved into the dining room. *Heavenly Father, please give me the right words. And, if it's not asking too much, please soften this man's heart toward my need.*

Stopping near his table, she cleared her throat to get his attention. "Excuse me, but can I speak to you for a moment?" Good—her voice hadn't squeaked like it sometimes did when she was nervous.

The man looked up from his nearly empty plate. "Ma'am?"

Her cheeks warmed as her courage wavered. What must he be thinking of her? Approaching him this way would have been considered bold if they were already acquainted. The fact that they were near strangers only made it that much more forward and unseemly.

But it was too late to turn back now. "Mr. Lassiter, is it?"

He nodded, his tobacco-brown eyes continuing to assess her. "That's right—Griff Lassiter."

"My name is Ruby Tuggle," she continued. "You might remember me from this morning?"

Not that *that* particular memory would lend her any additional credibility. She'd dropped a tray of dirty dishes practically at his feet in this very dining room. The man had been gentleman enough to help her collect the broken dishes and scattered cutlery. He'd even offered her a sympathetic smile when Mrs. Dowd had come out and given her a very public scolding for her clumsiness.

Then she realized she needed to get something straight before she continued. "This isn't about that," she said quickly, "though I do want to thank you again for your kindness. In fact, I don't work here anymore, so it's not hotel business at all. It's a personal matter I'm wanting to discuss with you." Realizing she was babbling, Ruby paused and took a steadying breath.

To her relief, Mr. Lassiter stood. She'd forgotten how very tall and imposing he was up close. The man commanded attention even when he wasn't trying to.

He waved her to the chair across from him. "Please have a seat. Can I order you something?"

Her spirits rose as she sat. This was a good beginning. He *was* a gentleman, and genuinely kind to boot. Now if only she could convince him to help her. "No, thank you. I've already eaten."

He took his seat, placed his elbows on the table and crossed his arms. "What can I do for you, Miss Tuggle?"

"I have a business proposition I'd like to discuss with you, if I may?"

That earned her a raised eyebrow. “I’m listening.”

“I understand you own a ranch in the Tyler area and will be returning there soon.”

He nodded. “I leave for Hawk’s Creek first thing in the morning.”

Her hands were clasped under the table so tight she felt the nails bite into her palms. This was it. “Well, I’m planning to travel to Tyler myself and I was wondering if I could hire you to provide me with an escort.” *Please, please, please say yes.*

There was a flash of surprise in his expression. “Excuse me for saying so, ma’am, but you don’t really know me. Wouldn’t you be more comfortable traveling with a relative or family friend?”

At least he hadn’t outright rejected her request. “I don’t have any family here.” Or anywhere else for that matter. “And no friends who could spare time for the trip.”

He studied her in silence for a long moment and she did her best not to fidget. Finally he leaned back in his chair. “Mind if I ask what kind of business you have in Tyler that would take you there on your own?”

She bristled a bit at that. It was really none of his business, after all. But she needed his goodwill so she swallowed her pride. “I plan to start a new life.” *A new life*—just saying that out loud lifted her spirits. No more facing so much resentment and pity. No more pretending she was happy here. “And I understand Tyler is a large enough place that I could find suitable work to support myself.”

He didn’t seem happy with her answer. “Miss

Tuggle, I hate to rain on your campfire, but it's really not wise for a young lady to strike out on her own like that. Especially in a strange place where she had no friends to turn to should the need arise. And finding suitable work, especially without someone to recommend you, might take time."

"I have enough money to tide me over for a bit." That had a satisfying sound to it, too. Discovering just yesterday that a nest egg had been set aside for her had made her almost giddy just imagining the possibilities. "I'm resourceful enough to take care of myself and I'm not afraid of hard or messy work."

He didn't appear convinced. "You mentioned you don't work here anymore. I don't mean to pry, but if this is just a reaction to that dust-up this morning, you'd likely be better off staying put and working things out with Mrs. Dowd."

Her heart sank as she saw her chances of success begin to fade. But she lifted her chin and tried again. "You're wrong if you think this is a spur of the moment decision. I've been planning to leave here for some time now. This morning's *dust-up,* as you call it, just gave me the final push is all. I'll be headed for Tyler tomorrow, with or without your company." That was partly bluster, of course. But she was just determined enough to contemplate doing it. It was past time to spread her wings.

"Ruby Anne, what do you think you're doing? Get up from there this minute."

Ruby jumped. She'd been so intent on making her

case to Mr. Lassiter that she hadn't heard Mrs. Dowd approach.

The stout rolling pin of a woman turned to Mr. Lassiter with an apologetic smile. "Sir, I'm so sorry if this girl has been bothering—"

"On the contrary."

Ruby, already halfway out of her chair, paused as her companion's voice cut across the woman's scold like a knife through lard.

"Miss Tuggle has graciously agreed to join me for dessert this evening," he continued, waving Ruby back down. "Speaking of which, I would appreciate it if you would please bring a bowl of your peach cobbler for each of us when you have a moment." While he hadn't raised his voice, and his expression remained pleasant, there was something in his tone that warned against argument.

Mrs. Dowd stiffened and her mouth snapped shut. Then she offered her best be-nice-to-the-customer smile. "Why, um, yes, of course. I'll get it for you at once."

The woman turned a sharper glance Ruby's way, but didn't linger.

Ruby had never seen Mrs. Dowd move so quickly. She turned to Mr. Lassiter with gratitude and a touch of awe. "Thank you."

He smiled. "It's just a bowl of cobbler."

Oh, it had been so much more than that. But he didn't give her time to elaborate.

"I can see you're determined," he said, returning to their original discussion. "But have you given any thought to the timing? Thanksgiving is a little over a week away and Christmas is right behind that. Surely you'll want to spend the holidays in familiar surroundings?"

She almost rolled her eyes at that. If he only knew. "Not at all. In fact, I believe being settled in a new place, surrounded by new people, is the perfect way to celebrate the holidays. It will definitely give me something extra to be thankful for."

That earned her another probing stare, which she endured without comment.

"How do you plan to travel?" he finally asked.

"I've purchased a small buggy and a horse," Ruby reported proudly. She'd taken care of that this morning as soon as she'd left the hotel. "I know having to match pace with a buggy will likely slow you down, but as I said, I'm prepared to pay you for your trouble."

He waved her offer aside. "That won't be an issue. I've acquired a young Angus bull today that I'm taking back to Hawk's Creek, so I'll be traveling slow and easy anyway."

Did that mean he was going to agree to her request? "Then you'll do it?"

He raised his napkin and smothered a cough.

She noticed again how tired he looked. "Are you okay?"

He shook his head dismissively. "It's just a bit of trail dust caught in my throat." He took a sip from his water glass, then leaned back again. "As for your other question, there's just one problem. I'm not going to Tyler proper. My ranch is a bit north of there, and since I'll have a bull tethered to my horse, I'd prefer to take the shortest route possible."

"I see." Ruby did her best to swallow her disappointment. Why hadn't he said so right away instead of letting her get her hopes up?

Saying she'd make the trip with or without him was one thing. Actually doing it was another. Not only were there the normal hazards of the road to worry about, but there was always the possibility of getting lost along the way. After all, since the ill-fated day when she'd arrived in Cleebit Springs at age seven, she hadn't traveled more than a mile outside of town.

So what did she do now?

Chapter Two

Griff took the opportunity brought about by Mrs. Dowd's reappearance to study the young woman seated across from him. A slip of a girl with dark hair and bright green eyes, with a face as readable as a babe's. It was hard to tell her age—she had an air of childlike trust about her that made her seem schoolgirlish—yet his instincts told him she was probably around eighteen or so.

Miss Tuggle also had an awkward coltishness about her that reminded him a little of his sister, Sadie. She seemed to have more than a touch of Sadie's stubbornness, as well.

The biggest problem in his opinion, though, was that she was much too trusting for her own good. Sure, *he'd* never take advantage of a young lady, but there were some who'd do it without a second thought. Especially after she'd blurted out that bit about having enough money to tide her over.

Yep, that ingenuousness of hers might be charming to a casual observer, but not to him. A girl like this could be a passel of trouble for whoever had the doubtful honor of looking out for her.

He just didn't want to be saddled with the job himself. He was tired, his head hurt and he had this new bull to get back to Hawk's Creek. The last thing he needed was to have to babysit some wide-eyed girl with big city dreams.

And while Ruby Tuggle was in no way his responsibility at the moment, he was irritated to realize that somehow she was well on her way to making herself so.

Because he kept coming back to the thought that if this had been Sadie…

"There now." Mrs. Dowd took a step back. "Is there anything else I can get for you?"

Griff glanced across the table. "Miss Tuggle?"

"No. I'm fine, thank you."

He was glad to see she didn't appear as nervous in the woman's presence as she had earlier.

He gave Mrs. Dowd a dismissive nod. "I think we're both fine for now."

As soon as the woman was gone, Miss Tuggle leaned forward. "Perhaps we could travel together for part of the way?"

Griff took a bite of his cobbler and had to follow it with a swallow of water. His throat was still scratchy. Hang it all, he just wanted to head upstairs and get a good night's rest. But he knew that wasn't going to happen if he didn't make sure this fool girl didn't go off on her own tomorrow and get herself lost—or worse.

"Actually, I have a better idea."

"Oh?"

He mentally winced at the sudden hope that flared in her expression. This girl was so transparent. "Since you seem so determined to leave here—"

She nodded vigorously. "Oh, I am."

"At the pace I'll be moving tomorrow it'll take all of nine hours to get to Cornerstone, which is where we would part ways for you to go on to Tyler and me to go to the ranch. That means it would be dusk at best before you actually reach your destination." Assuming she could make it on her own at all. "Which wouldn't give you a whole lot of time to find accommodations for yourself and your horse and buggy before full nightfall."

"Surely there would be someone in town who could direct me to a hotel or boardinghouse."

Did she think everyone in the world was as helpful—or as honest—as her neighbors here in Cleebit Springs? She'd learn different soon enough. "Still, much better for you to arrive in the morning when you're well rested. Easier to get your bearings and be a mite more selective about your accommodations."

Her brow drew down in a thoughtful expression. "I hadn't thought of that."

Of course she hadn't. More proof that she had no idea what she was in for. "There's a church in Cornerstone and the reverend and his wife have been known to provide shelter to travelers when it's needed. What

I propose is that I escort you that far and you spend the night with them. Then the next morning either I or one of my ranch hands can escort you into Tyler and see you safely settled in."

Her face lit up. "What a wonderful plan. Oh, I knew you were a true gentleman."

Griff resisted the urge to roll his eyes as he smothered another cough in his napkin. Something about this still didn't feel right. "Isn't there someone I should be talking to or asking permission of to take you on this trip? I know you said you don't have any family here, but surely there's someone who looks out for you? I mean, whom do you live with?"

She drew herself up as if he'd offended her. "I'll have you know I'm an adult—I turned twenty last week. I live over at the boardinghouse and I look out for myself."

Griff was too tired to take this any further. He set his napkin on the table. So she was older than he'd thought. That still didn't make her capable of getting along on her own. "I'd like to get an early start in the morning. Do you think you can be ready at seven o'clock?"

Her indignation immediately turned to smiles. "That won't be a problem. But there is one other thing I should mention."

What now? "And that is?" From the way she hesitated, it was a good bet he wasn't going to like it.

"I plan to take my cat with me," she finally blurted out.

"Cat?" He didn't think much of cats other than as varmint catchers for the barn.

"Yes. Patience is well behaved—mostly, anyway. She won't be any trouble, I promise. You don't mind, do you?"

Patience? Sounded like some fluffy, pampered house pet. "As long as you understand I don't aim to go chasing after the critter if it runs off."

"Oh, I wouldn't expect you to."

"Then I don't see a problem." He stood. "Now, if there's nothing else, we have a long day ahead of us tomorrow, so if you'll excuse me, I think I'll retire for the evening. I suggest you do the same."

She scrambled to her feet. "Of course. And again, let me say how very grateful I am."

A few minutes later Griff sat on a chair in his room, pulling off his boots. What he wouldn't give to be back at Hawk's Creek right now, in his own room, headed to his own bed.

His own very large, very comfortable, but just as lonely bed.

He shook his head in disgust as he put his left boot on the floor beside his chair and started tugging on the right one. This restless self-pity that had been creeping up on him these past few months was both pointless and beneath him.

He supposed being with the Lipscoms today out at the Double Bar L Ranch had triggered this mood. The family consisted of Barney Lipscom, his wife, his son, his daughter-in-law and three grandkids. When his business with Barney had concluded, Barney had insisted Griff take his noon meal with them. It had given Griff an up-close view of their lives together.

The conversation at the table had been lively, the affection between the family members apparent. Both Mary and Amy were strong women with lives deeply rooted in their family and in the family ranch. They seemed equally at home in the kitchen as in the barn.

And he'd found himself more than a little jealous. It was the kind of life he longed for. Instead, he shared his large home with Inez, the housekeeper and cook who'd been at Hawk's Creek since before he was born. He loved her as he would a favorite aunt, but she was no substitute for a wife.

To have a wife who would be a proper helpmeet to him, one who loved the rancher's life as much as he did, and with whom he could share, if not love, then a mutual respect.

Was that too much to ask?

Apparently so, since his two attempts had resulted in sound rejection. The ladies in question had eventually decided ranch life was not for them.

Or maybe it was just that *he* wasn't right for them.

Griff tossed his boot across the room, irritated at the direction his thoughts had taken. Self-pity was not productive and definitely not very dignified. If it was his lot in life to face it alone, so be it. Wishing it different wouldn't make it so.

As Griff climbed into bed a few minutes later, his thoughts turned back to Miss Tuggle. If her story was to be believed, it seemed she was even more alone in life than he was. At least he had Inez.

Of course, he wasn't completely convinced she wasn't exaggerating or embellishing on her situation.

Young girls seemed prone to do that. Still, he'd given her his word.

He punched his pillow into a more comfortable shape.

Escorting a head-in-the-clouds girl and her fluffy cat…

Just what in the world had he let himself in for?

Griff stepped out of the hotel the next morning in a sour mood. He hadn't slept well and his muscles were stiff and sore. The cold, dreary weather that greeted him didn't help much. All in all, not a good time to be undertaking a long trip on horseback.

True to her word, Miss Tuggle was sitting in her buggy parked outside the hotel, waiting for him.

"Good morning," she said, her expression as bright as that of a kid on Christmas morning. Obviously the prospect of the weather conditions and the length of their upcoming journey didn't dampen her mood any. Or maybe she just didn't know enough to be worried.

But he'd been brought up to be civil. "Good morning. I—"

He paused when he spotted the cat perched beside her. Instead of the well-groomed, well-fed feline he'd expected, this scraggly critter with a coat as gray and mottled as the overcast sky could have easily been mistaken for a stray.

"This is Patience," she said proudly. Then she gave him an apologetic smile. "I'm afraid she doesn't like strangers very much so it might be best if you don't try to pet her."

Now why in the world would he want to pet that scruffy-looking thing? "That won't be a problem."

She nodded and sat up straighter. "We're both ready whenever you are."

"Give me just a few minutes." Griff examined her horse and worn-looking carriage closely—the last thing he needed was to have the horse give out or the vehicle break down on them somewhere out on the road. Especially the way he was feeling this morning. The scratch in his throat was still there and the coffee and biscuits he'd had for breakfast sat heavy in his stomach. He'd be glad to get back to Hawk's Creek, and the comfort of familiar surroundings. And truth to tell, a little cosseting from Inez would be welcome, as well.

One thing he did notice while he was checking her equipment was that, though the buggy was a bit roomier than most vehicles of its type, she was traveling light. The only luggage she had with her was one not-very-large trunk. Did it contain the sum total of her possessions? Or was she literally leaving her old life behind?

Finally satisfied that the horse and vehicle were both sound enough to make the trip, Griff nodded and stepped back.

"It'll do. I need to collect my animals from the livery. Meet me there in a few minutes."

Twenty minutes later he had the bull tethered to the back of the buggy and had loaded a bag of feed in the carriage boot. He climbed up on his horse, gathered the reins and glanced at his traveling companion. She seemed, as Inez liked to say, happy as a pup chasing a stick. Even as he felt the urge to roll his eyes, a reluctant smile tugged at his lips. He supposed he should let her enjoy herself while she could. No doubt her cheery mood would evaporate by the time they were an hour or so into what promised to be a tedious, cold and dreary trip. "Ready?"

She nodded. "I've been ready for this day for ages."

He just didn't understand why big cities held such appeal for some folk. Give him wide-open land any day. "All right, then. Match your pace to mine. And remember, that's valuable livestock tied to your buggy—I don't want to wear him out before I get him to Hawk's Creek."

She nodded again. "Just lead the way."

He pulled his hat down more firmly as he set his horse in motion. Not only were the skies overcast this morning, but there was a nip in the air that hadn't been there yesterday. No hint of rain yet, though. Maybe they'd get lucky and this would be the worst of it.

He watched her closely as they set out, prepared to intervene if she wasn't mindful of his bull. But after ten minutes he relaxed.

"Tell me about this ranch of yours," she asked. "Hawk's Creek, is it?"

"That's right. Some of the richest pasture land in all of Texas—rolling hills, several springs that run practically year-round, lush grazing, prime timber. There's no other place like it. It's been in my family for three generations." And now it was down to him.

"So you've lived there all your life."

"Yep. And I plan to die there, as well." No city—big or small—for him. His roots were planted in Hawk's Creek land and he didn't think he could flourish anywhere else. "What about you? You live in Cleebit Springs your entire life?"

"Most of it. I arrived there when I was seven years old and stayed put until today."

"And now you want to move to Tyler."

She shrugged and kept her gaze on the road. "I'm just ready for a change."

Another restless spirit? Like his brother, Ry. And Belle, his first love. And Martha, his second.

"Do you have any family?" she asked, pulling him out of his thoughts.

He noticed she was quick to turn the discussion away from herself. "An older brother and younger sister—Ry and Sadie."

"I always wanted siblings." Her tone was wistful. "But my mother died when I was three and my father never remarried." She glanced back his way. "I guess the three of you live on that ranch together, like a real family."

He shook his head as he raised a hand to smother a series of chest-tightening coughs. "Both Ry and Sadie moved on," he said when he'd caught his breath again. "Ry left a long time ago, back when we were both still teens. Went to live in Philadelphia with our grandfather." It had been hard when his big brother chose life back East over life on the ranch, and it had driven a wedge between the two of them, a wedge that had only recently been dislodged when Ry married Josie and moved back to Texas.

"And your sister?"

That was another move he hadn't seen coming. "Sadie got married last year, to a fellow who moved to Texas from New York. It was a whirlwind kind of thing. And, as it turns out, both she and Ry ended up in the same town—Knotty Pine. It's about sixty miles southeast of the ranch." He tried not to be jealous of their closeness. And their newfound happiness.

"So you live alone now?"

He shifted in the saddle, suddenly annoyed with all her questions. "Inez is there."

"Inez?"

"Inez Garner—I guess you'd call her our housekeeper. But she's more than that, more like part of the family. Inez has been at Hawk's Creek since before I was born—I can't imagine the place without her. After my ma died she was the glue that helped hold us all together."

"She sounds like a special lady."

"That she is." Enough of answering her questions—time to ask a few of his own. "What about you? You said you don't have any family—who raised you?"

Was it his imagination or did some of her cheeriness ebb? Maybe he shouldn't have brought up her orphaned status.

"I reckon you could say just about everybody in Cleebit Springs had a hand in raising me," she answered. "After they buried my father—I was seven at the time—the whole community banded together to make certain I was provided for. Different families took turns looking out for me."

Close-knit communities were like that, he supposed—doing what they could to help their neighbors when there was a need. So why was she so eager to give all that up? Seemed shortsighted at best, ungrateful at worst. "Sounds to me as if you had a very large foster family."

"I suppose you could look at it that way."

She didn't seem much taken with the idea. "Folks don't have to be blood kin to be family," he offered. "Inez and I are proof of that."

She gave a noncommittal nod, keeping her gaze straight ahead.

"Might be you'll miss the folks in Cleebit Springs more than you think you will," he said, trying again. "You're going to find out soon enough that folks in large towns tend to mind their own business more often than not and aren't always as neighborly as those in smaller towns."

She shrugged. "Folks minding their own business isn't such a bad thing."

He supposed some lessons had to be learned from experience. And it seemed for her this was going to be one of them.

He only hoped she didn't get hurt too badly when she learned it.

Ruby was glad Mr. Lassiter didn't press further. There was no way she'd agree to call those folks back in Cleebit Springs her family, but she didn't want to speak ill of them, either. Her daddy had taught her to always look for the good in any person or situation, and she'd tried to honor his memory by doing just that. It had been so hard in those first few weeks after he was taken from her, when she'd been dealing with the shock of his sudden, horrific death, when she'd been surrounded by people she didn't know, when the nightmares had come night after night.

But in time the shock, if not the memories, had faded, the people had become more familiar, the nightmares had come less frequently. And that was when her upbringing had kicked in. She'd stopped crying and forced herself to look for any silver lining she could find, in fact had made a game of it.

But even on the best of those days, she hadn't thought of anyone in Cleebit Springs as family. There were lots of good folks there, she knew that. It's just that her memories and relationships with them were all colored by her father's death. Whether right or wrong, she was genuinely happy to know that from this day forward she'd never have to face any of them again. The farther away from Cleebit Springs they got, the lighter her spirits. It had been thirteen long, lonely years since she'd felt so buoyant.

After the silence had dragged on for a bit, Ruby decided it was time for something a bit more cheerful. "Tell me about Tyler."

"I guess it's a fine city, as cities go anyway. What do you want to know about it?"

"Everything." She was determined to look on this as a grand adventure—no matter how discouraging his tone. “Start with what I can expect to find when I get there.”

“Well, let’s see, there are sawmills, an ice factory, a cotton gin and some fruit-packing plants. There are several other factories, but I don’t guess you’re much interested in that sort of thing.”

“I want to know about *all* of it. I’m going to be looking for work when I get there, remember?”

“All right. Besides the mills and factories, there are stores and shops, some of them huge brick buildings with three floors of merchandise, where you can find just about anything from dry goods to flowers, from hardware to fine jewelry.”

He rolled his shoulders. “And there are churches of course, big ones and small ones of just about any denomination you can imagine. There’s a busy railway station there along with shipping and freight companies. Oh, and most of the businesses and many of the homes have electricity.”

“Mercy! Do the boardinghouses have electricity?”

“I’ve never visited one, but I imagine they do.”

She looked down at her cat. “Did you hear that, Patience? Won’t that be a fine thing?”

The cat’s only response was a lazy blink.

“I wouldn’t call it fine—much too noisy and crowded.”

She refused to let her mood be dampened—this was her chance to build a brand-new life, to prove to herself that she could stand on her own. Because she had no one else to depend on. “Crowds don’t bother me. What else is there?”

"There's a lot more." His tone indicated he wasn't overly impressed with the list he was reciting. "A courthouse, several hotels, lots of eating places from small cafés to fancy restaurants."

Another fit of coughing interrupted his litany. "If you're interested in more refined offerings," he continued, "there are schools and a library, a newspaper office, two opera houses, a theater and some uppity-sounding social clubs."

Uppity, huh? Did he think that's what she was looking for? But the library—now that *did* sound interesting. She loved to read, but her choices had been limited. Many of the families she'd stayed with had either not had any reading material or had not thought it an appropriate pastime for her. She had exactly three books to her name, safely packed in her trunk. All three had belonged to her father—a Bible, a book about plants and a copy of Mark Twain's *The Prince and The Pauper.* All were dog-eared from the many times she'd read them.

"Sounds like a mighty fine place." She looked over at him. "Do you visit there often?"

"Once or twice a month. Mostly for supplies or to meet the train." He grimaced. "It's much too crowded for my taste. And besides, there's lots to keep me busy at Hawk's Creek."

Interesting how his voice and expression took on a whole different tone when he spoke of his ranch—deeper, more relaxed. She wondered if he was even aware of how telling that was.

"I don't think I'll mind the crowds so much," she

replied. "It sounds like a marvelous place to start a new life."

They rode along in silence for a few minutes, then she cleared her throat. "That's a fine-looking horse you've got there. Does he have a name?"

"Chester." He scowled. "Are you always this chatty?"

Oh, my—he sounded irritable. Probably as much to do with that cough of his as with her. She gave him an apologetic smile. "Actually, no. But since I'm starting out on a new adventure, I find myself full of questions. Sorry if I'm bothering you."

"Sometimes a fella just likes to take a break from talking and hear his own thoughts for a while."

"Of course."

He dropped back to check on the bull and she looked down at Patience, who was now sitting on the floor of the buggy. "Well, at least I have you to talk to."

The cat gave her a long-suffering look, then went back to grooming itself.

"You, too? Well, neither one of you gloomy glumps are going to dampen my mood. It's a wonderful day, just chock-full of silver linings, and I aim to enjoy each and every one of them."

Chapter Three

Griff called a halt around noon. He'd regretted his earlier sour comment within a few minutes of uttering it. After all, it was only natural for Miss Tuggle to be curious about what her future might hold.

The fact that she didn't seem at all cowed by his set-down surprised him. She made occasional comments to her cat, hummed now and then as if she couldn't contain her exuberance and just generally maintained a cheerful demeanor. There didn't seem to be much that could dampen her spirits.

But it'd been a long morning and she *had* quieted considerably these past thirty minutes. Though she hadn't complained, he figured Miss Tuggle was probably ready to get out of that buggy and move around a bit.

"I don't know about you," he said with a smile, "but I'm ready to have a look at what's in that basket you packed."

Her face lit up. "That sounds lovely."

He had the fleeting impression that she was referring as much to the fact that he'd spoken first as to the opportunity to get out of the buggy. "The road widens up ahead by that big oak," he continued. "Why don't we pull the buggy up under the tree and stretch our legs for a little while?"

Within a few minutes he was handing her down. She was surprisingly light and agile. Strange that he hadn't really noticed her eyes before—such a vivid shade of green, flecked with sparks of gold.

He took a moment to steady her once her feet were on the ground and, just for a moment, their gazes locked. Then her cat sprang down and landed at their feet, and the moment passed.

She quickly turned back to the buggy. "I'll get the hamper. It's right—"

He stopped her with a touch to her arm. "Let me get that."

She stepped aside. "Of course." Then she turned away. "I'd better keep an eye on Patience."

"It's been my experience that cats aren't much good at coming when called."

She laughed. "True. But I think she'll stay close when she sees what's in the hamper."

As he stepped back with the hamper, he noticed she was hugging herself. It was definitely colder now than it had been earlier. They probably should make this stop a quick one. The sooner they reached their destination, the better.

She stepped forward and reached inside the buggy. "I also packed a blanket we can sit on while we eat."

"Good thinking." He took her arm to help her over the uneven ground. "It's not exactly picnic weather, but we won't be here long anyway."

He set the hamper beside the tree. "If you can get things set up here, I'm going to give the animals some feed."

"Of course."

By the time he'd given the bull and the two horses each a bit of oats, she had the blanket spread out and had pulled some tin cups and plates out of the hamper. The cat sat beside her, tail swishing slowly, eyeing the hamper as if it were a mouse hole.

Miss Tuggle looked up as he joined her. "I'm afraid the food's not anything fancy, but it should be filling enough."

"No need to apologize. It was good of you to bring anything at all." Besides, he wasn't very hungry. "So, what do we have?"

She started itemizing things as she pulled them out of the hamper. "Some boiled ham slices, a wedge of cheese, two boiled eggs, a couple of biscuits and four nice ripe persimmons."

The cat swiped a paw in the direction of the ham, but Miss Tuggle was faster. She scooped up the cat, holding the affronted feline away from the food. "Oh, no you don't. Wait your turn."

She turned back to Griff, her hand stroking the cat's head. "There's a jug of apple cider in the hamper to wash it down with."

It seemed she'd gone to a lot of trouble. He hoped his lack of appetite didn't hurt her feelings.

She handed him a plate and smiled uncertainly. "Before we start, would you like to say grace?"

Griff paused in the act of reaching for a biscuit. He was embarrassed that he'd gotten out of the habit of praying before meals since Sadie had moved away. Perhaps it was time he remedied that.

He bowed his head. "Thank You, Father, for this food set before us, and for the many other blessings You provide to us each day. Watch over us as we travel. And watch over Miss Tuggle as she begins her new life in Tyler. May she find whatever it is she's looking for."

His companion added an "Amen," then smiled up at him.

Griff pointed to the squirming cat in her arms. "Is that varmint going to let you eat?"

She laughed. "As long as she gets her share. Don't worry, I packed enough." She quickly broke off several slivers of ham and some crumbles of cheese and set them on the corner of the blanket. The cat sashayed over and began eating the morsels as if getting served first were her right.

Griff shook his head. Despite the cat's disreputable appearance, it seemed it was a pampered pet after all.

He turned back to his own plate and cautiously looked over the food. His stomach rebelled at the idea of the ham or the cheese, but he knew he ought to eat something before they got back on the road. He carefully selected one of the biscuits and an egg.

Miss Tuggle frowned when she saw his skimpily loaded plate. "Oh, dear, don't you like ham and cheese? I should have asked ahead of time. Or is it Patience? If cats bother you I can—"

He held up a hand. She might be an overly cheery girl, but she was also quick to accept blame unnecessarily, as well. "I do like ham and cheese. And your cat isn't bothering me. I'm just not very hungry, is all."

"Oh." She was quiet for a while but he could see her worry as she studied him. When he coughed again, she frowned. "Are you sure you're okay? Maybe the folks at one of those farmhouses we passed a ways back would—"

"It's just a cough. I'm fine."

She slipped the cat another sliver of ham. "I lived with Doc Mulligan's family a couple of years ago. He always said a deep cough like yours should be treated right away or it could lead to something really serious."

"That might be true for some folk. But sometimes a cough is just a cough. I haven't been sick enough to slow me down since I lost my first tooth." He lifted the jug out of the hamper. "Hand me those cups and I'll pour us some of this cider." Hopefully she'd get the message that the subject of his health was closed.

She did as he asked and waited until he finished pouring to speak again. "So, did you travel all the way to Cleebit Springs just to fetch that bull?"

At least she'd decided to drop the subject of his health. "Actually, I hadn't planned on getting a new bull at all. I had some business to take care of with Barney Lipscom over at the Double Bar L Ranch."

He forced himself to eat another bite of biscuit, then washed it down with a swig of cider. "Barney's been experimenting with Angus bloodlines and was excited about the results he's gotten. He insisted I take one of his young bulls to see for myself."

"That was generous of him. You must be good friends."

"He and my pa were." Griff noticed she'd finished up her meal. "If you're done, we should get back on the road. Sorry we can't make this a longer stop, but I don't like the looks of the weather. The sooner we get to where we're going, the better."

"Of course." She scrambled to her knees, then looked around with a frown. "Now where did Patience get off to?"

Griff stood, eyes scanning the tree line. "She can't have gone far—she was just here."

Miss Tuggle stood as well, biting her lower lip. "I should've watched her closer."

Now what did he do? He'd told her he wouldn't go chasing after her cat, but what if the four-legged troublemaker didn't return in the next few minutes? Could he get Miss Tuggle to go on without her pet? "I don't suppose the critter is trained to come when you call."

She shook her head, then pushed a lock of hair behind her ear with fingers that trembled. "Oh, if something's happened to her—"

Good grief, she wasn't going to cry, was she? "No need to get all worked up just yet," he said quickly.

"Why don't you pack up things here and I'll take a quick look around."

"Thank you." She offered him a grateful smile, but the worry never left her expression.

Swallowing a few choice words, he stepped away from the blanket and let his eyes scan the tree line once again. He didn't hold out much hope of finding the feline, though, not unless it wanted to be found. A moment later he got his first clue as to the animal's whereabouts when he heard the excited barking of a dog. It sounded close. Maybe the threat of a dog on its trail would send the cat scampering back in this direction.

"Do you hear that?" Miss Tuggle was at his elbow, the folded blanket in her arms.

"Yes. Don't worry. I'm sure your cat can outrun most dogs. Probably streak out of those woods any minute now."

"She *is* fast."

A moment later Griff frowned. The tenor of the barking had changed. The dog no longer seemed to be moving and it sounded more like baying, as if it had treed its quarry.

Great. Just great.

Griff headed off in the direction of the barking.

Ruby's chin came up. He hadn't really invited her to follow him, but there was no way she was going to stay behind—Patience was, after all, *her* cat. She did her best to keep up with him, but it wasn't easy. His long legs ate up the ground with amazing speed.

Fortunately they didn't have far to go. Just inside the tree line they encountered the dog who was making all that racket. The black-and-brown hound had its front legs braced up against a tree trunk, nose pointed heavenward and howling up a storm.

Oh, dear, was poor Patience up there somewhere?

As soon as the dog spotted them it stopped barking and dropped back down on all fours. Griff put a hand up and Ruby obediently stopped.

He moved forward, slowly, speaking to the animal in a tone too soft for her to make out the words. After a moment the dog's tail began to wag and Mr. Lassiter was able to stoop down and ruffle the animal's fur.

While her companion was busy winning over the dog, Ruby anxiously scanned the almost bare branches of the tree. She finally caught sight of a furry face peering down at her from what must be a good ten feet above her head. "Look, there she is."

Mr. Lassiter glanced at her, then upward. "It figures," he said drily. "Wouldn't do for her to stop on a lower branch, would it?"

He stood and stared down at the dog, pointing away from the tree. "Get along now."

Ruby grinned as the animal cocked its head to one side, as if trying to figure out if this was some sort of game.

"Get!" He said it more firmly and louder this time, stomping his foot for emphasis.

The dog spun and loped away a few paces before turning back to stare at him.

Mr. Lassiter let out an exasperated breath. "Mutt, I really don't have the time or patience for this."

As if the animal finally understood, it turned and ran back into the woods.

Mr. Lassiter turned to her. "I hope that animal of yours will come when called after all."

She hoped so, too. Moving forward until she was directly under the branch Patience clung to, Ruby set the picnic blanket down and made a downward motion with her hand. "Patience, come on down, sweetie. That big bad dog is gone now, so it's safe."

She kept her gaze on the cat, ignoring Mr. Lassiter's snort at her description of the dog as big and bad. But Patience still didn't budge. "I won't let anything hurt you, I promise. Just come on down so we can get on the road again."

What was she going to do if the cat refused to come down right away? She would never abandon her pet, but would Mr. Lassiter go off and leave them? She tried calling Patience again, letting some of her desperation creep into her tone.

Finally Mr. Lassiter stepped forward. "Enough."

Ruby turned to him, trying to gain a little more time. "Please. She can't stay up there forever. I can go back to the hamper and get a bit of ham. Maybe I can tempt her—"

"I doubt that'll work. And we've already wasted too much time."

"But I can't just leave her here. She needs me." *And I need her, because without her I'd be totally alone.*

"Nobody said anything about leaving her." He

tossed his hat on top of the picnic blanket, then, despite the chilly temperature, shrugged out of his jacket. “Here, hold this.”

She took the jacket and hugged it against her chest, its warmth strangely comforting. “What are you going to do?” A dozen scenarios played out in her head—everything from him throwing rocks at her poor pet to him climbing up after it.

He momentarily paused in the act of rolling up his sleeves and raised a brow. “What do you *think* I'm going to do?”

She decided to believe the best of him and his intentions. “Go up after her?”

Instead of responding he finished rolling up his sleeves, took his jacket back from her and moved to the tree.

“But—” She missed the feel of his jacket in her arms. “You said you weren't going to chase after her.”

“And I'm not.” He gave her a considering look as he tied the jacket's sleeves in a chunky knot around his waist. “Are you trying to talk me out of this?”

“No. I just…” He really *was* going to climb up after Patience. The man was a real-life hero. “Please be careful.”

He nodded. “Just be prepared for what comes next. I don't aim to climb back down with that critter spitting and clawing in my arms.”

Now what did he mean by that? Ruby watched as he grabbed a lower limb and tested its weight. “I must be out of my mind,” he muttered. “I haven't climbed a tree since I was a scrawny kid.”

She had trouble picturing him as a scrawny anything. Especially right now, what with the way his muscles bunched beneath his shirt as he grabbed hold of one of the lower branches.

Within seconds he was hauling himself up into the network of skeletal limbs. A heartbeat later he was standing on a lower branch and looking for footing on the next tier up. For a big man, he was surprisingly agile. She couldn't help but admire the relative ease with which he maneuvered his way up the tree.

When he paused to control another bout of coughs, however, she had to bite her lip to keep from warning him once again to be careful.

Please God, don't let him fall. I'd never forgive myself if he got hurt because of me and Patience.

But the cough quieted and he continued as if nothing had happened. When he finally reached a branch that put him level with Patience, Mr. Lassiter leaned with his back against the trunk and carefully untied his jacket from about his waist.

She wished she could see what was going on better. "Is Patience okay?"

"She seems fine." His tone held very little sympathy for the object of his rescue.

"Try talking softly to her," Ruby urged. "She's probably scared to death, poor thing." If he'd only handle Patience the same soothing way he had the dog earlier—

Before she could finish that thought, he'd thrown his coat over the cat, scooped her up and had her bundled as cleanly as if he'd tossed her in a sack.

Not that Patience was taking it without a fight. The poor thing was screeching loud enough to be heard for miles and she was writhing so wildly that Ruby wondered how Mr. Lassiter was managing to keep his balance.

"Be careful." She hadn't been able to contain the warning this time. "How are you going to climb back down carrying Patience?"

"I'm not."

What did he mean? Had he gone to all this trouble just to leave—

"Move a little to your left and get ready to catch."

"Catch? Surely you're not going to *drop* her."

"That's exactly what I'm going to do. Don't worry, she won't break. Just make sure you hold on to the critter and don't let her run off again."

"But I—"

"Ready or not."

And with that, the bundle of squirming, screeching feline came falling from above. Ruby managed to catch it, but the impact knocked her down on her backside. She maintained a tight hold on the bundle but quickly unwrapped it enough to free Patience's head.

"There now, that's better, isn't it?" she cooed. "You just go ahead and spit and howl all you want—you've had a rough time of it and deserve to be upset. Yes, yes, go ahead, protest as loud and indignantly as you like." She continued crooning to her pet, not trying to hush her, merely reassure her.

When she finally looked up, Mr. Lassiter stood a few feet away, staring at her curiously.

When their eyes met he stepped forward and held out a hand to help her up. "Are you okay?"

"I'm fine." She gave Patience a quick hug before accepting his hand. "We both are." Once she was on her feet, they stood face-to-face for a moment, still holding hands. "I don't know how to thank you," she said softly. "That's the kindest thing anyone's ever done for me."

Something flashed in his expression—surprise, sympathy, something else? She couldn't be sure, but she felt the lightest of squeezes to her hand before he dropped it.

"You're welcome, Miss Tuggle. Now—"

"Please, call me Ruby." Her face warmed at her brashness, but she pressed on. "I mean, you've been so kind and I feel that we've become friends, and Miss Tuggle just sounds so formal."

"All right, *Ruby*. And you can call me Griff."

Griff. She liked that. It had a strong, honest quality to it. Heroic. Just like the man.

"Now, as I started to say, we've tarried long enough. We better get going."

"Of course." Her hand still felt the comforting warmth of his touch.

Mr. Lassi—*Griff* turned to retrieve his hat and he grabbed up the blanket, as well.

"I'll get the hamper," he said, slapping his hat on his head. "You just make sure that animal of yours gets in the buggy."

She smiled and turned back toward the carriage. He might pretend to be gruff and dour, but he wasn't fooling her. The man had the heart of a hero.

Chapter Four

Griff rubbed his chin as he watched Ruby move toward the buggy, cat in hand. She was still crooning to the critter, as if it were a hurt child in need of comfort.

The woman was overly sentimental about her pet, not to mention starry-eyed and seriously infected with wanderlust. None of those qualities were ones that would endear her to him—he preferred someone with a more realistic, practical outlook. But he couldn't shake the memory of the look in her eyes just now when she'd thanked him and declared his rescue of her pet the kindest thing anyone had ever done for her. Something about her look and tone at that moment had tugged at him, had made his irritation seem suddenly petty.

She stopped by the hamper and he watched her stoop to reach inside. Pulling out some ham, she fed a sliver to her cat. "This ought to make you feel better," she said in that same lilting tone suitable for a nursery. "Once we get in the buggy I'll give you the rest."

He rolled his eyes, putting down his earlier feeling to a side effect of that irritating cough that had him all out of sorts. His first impression had been the right one—the girl was just plain unprepared for the world she was so desperate to enter.

He grabbed the hamper and followed her to the buggy. By the time he caught up with them, the cat was crouched beneath the buggy seat, chewing on another bit of ham as if nothing out of the ordinary had just happened.

Ruby turned to him with a smile. "I think Patience will be fine now. Oh, here's your jacket."

Griff set the hamper in the buggy then took his coat from her. He shook it out and examined it, frowning at the half-dozen rips in the lining.

Ruby followed his gaze and gave a little cry. "Oh, dear, I'm so sorry—Patience was quite naughty. Naturally I'll pay to have it replaced."

"That won't be necessary. I'm sure Inez can patch it up for me." The sooner this journey was done the happier he'd be. He jammed his arms in the sleeves then offered her his hand. "Now, up you go. The sky's looking more overcast by the minute and we need to make tracks."

"Of course."

He made quick work of handing her up, taking care not to let his hands linger.

She gathered up the reins, her expression mirroring his concern. "You're right about the weather looking gloomy. We'll likely run into rain soon and getting soaked isn't going to do that cough of yours any good." She patted the seat. "Why don't you ride up here with me where there's at least a little protection from the elements? There's more than enough room."

"Thanks for the offer, but it's not raining yet. We might get lucky and miss it altogether. Besides I want to keep an eye on that bull. I can't watch him if I'm inside the buggy."

"What if I let you handle the reins? Then you can go just as slow and easy as you like."

As if there was any question but that he'd take the reins if he climbed in. "Thanks, but I'll ride Chester awhile longer." He stepped back, but then noticed her shoulders flutter. Was she cold? With a frown, he reached back into the buggy and plucked out the picnic cloth, placing it on the seat beside her. "Here, use this as an extra lap blanket."

She held it out. "Maybe you should—"

He didn't let her finish. "Don't argue. I'm used to being out in all sorts of weather—cows and fences need to be tended to year-round—so this bit of nastiness doesn't bother me."

Despite his reassurances to her, Griff eyed the horizon worriedly. Besides being markedly colder, there was a dampness in the air now that didn't bode well for his hope of staying dry. And worse yet, he knew he wasn't quite as okay as he'd tried to convince her. He was coughing more often now and that general achiness had settled into his bones.

He just needed to get home to Hawk's Creek. Inez would take it from there. But first, he had to get Ruby Tuggle safely delivered to Reverend Martin at Cornerstone.

Using the buggy's step, he reached up to loosen the side panels. "In fact, I'm going to fasten down the sides. If it *does* start raining, you'll be better protected."

It would also make conversation between them more difficult.

Now why didn't that thought please him as much as it would have when they'd set out this morning?

He mounted his horse and gave her the signal to set the buggy in motion. By his reckoning they had another four hours of travel ahead of them. And that was assuming they didn't make any more stops or encounter delays. There was no way the rain was going to hold off that long.

Sure enough, thirty minutes later he felt the first drop of rain. It was isolated for the moment, but it wouldn't be for much longer. The urge to move faster was strong but he couldn't do it as long as he had that bull to transport.

Clenching his jaw, he reached a decision. Maneuvering his horse closer to the buggy, he claimed Ruby's attention. "There's a farmhouse just up the road a bit. I'm going to ride on ahead to talk to the owner if you think you'll be okay for a few minutes on your own."

"I'll be fine."

He felt as if he were abandoning her. Ridiculous,

because it was straight ahead less than half a mile. "Keep at this pace and pull over by the barn when you get there. All right?"

This time she merely nodded and to his surprise didn't ask any questions about what he was up to.

By the time the buggy caught up with him, he'd struck a deal with the farmer, a man by the name of Fred Callums who had been blessed with an army of children. Griff had counted at least eight faces peering out from various windows and doors before he lost count. Mr. Callums seemed quite eager to care for the bull for the next few days in return for the five dollars Griff offered him. No doubt money was scarce in this very full household.

Within minutes of Ruby's arrival, the bull was untied and led to a paddock by one of Mr. Callums's boys, and Griff had handed over the bag of oats and the money to the farmer himself, along with a promise to send someone to fetch the animal in the next day or two.

He turned to his traveling companion. "If you don't mind, I think I'm ready to take you up on that offer to ride in the buggy."

"Of course."

Was that a hint of relief in her smile? He tied Chester to the back of the buggy where the bull had been a few minutes ago, then climbed up next to her. The cat let out an indignant yowl at being disturbed. So much for the varmint's gratitude for Griff's rescue.

Ruby immediately reached down to pet the animal with a "Hush now" command while Griff matched the cat's glare with one of his own, and the animal finally subsided.

Griff released the brake and gave the reins a flick. "Now, let's see if we can make a little better time."

"That was a good idea, finding a place to stable your bull."

Griff shrugged. "That's one less thing to have to worry about if this storm gets worse." He cut a glance her way. "I'd thought that I might ask them to put you up for the night as well, but when I saw how many were in that household I didn't think you'd be very comfortable there."

She gave him a reassuring smile. "I don't mind sleeping in a barn if it comes to that, but you're right, it would have put them out to have yet another person to look after." He noticed her chin tilt up slightly. "And I'm not as fragile as you seem to think. Short of ice and hail, I'll survive a bit of wet winter weather just fine."

He certainly hoped she was right—he wouldn't want her to get sick while she was under his care.

She reached for the blanket that was over her lap. "Speaking of which, I have two of these. Why don't you take one?"

He waved the offer aside. "Keep it. I'm fine for now."

No way was he going to let her mollycoddle him, especially at the expense of her own comfort.

Ruby compressed her lips in a worried line. It had been nearly an hour since they'd left the Callums place and so far the dark clouds had only managed to produce a light drizzle. But her companion was not looking good. He sat hunched in his seat and his cough was painful to listen to. She'd asked twice again if he wanted to use one of the blankets, but he'd been almost brusque in his refusal. Was it a matter of pride with him? Or did he truly not realize how sick he was?

When the next coughing spasm overtook him she'd had enough. She pulled the top blanket off her lap and firmly placed it on his.

Mr. Lassiter shot her an irritated look, but she glared right back. To her relief he finally nodded and issued a curt "Thank you."

She sensed the weariness beneath his irritation and so refused to take offense. "Would you like me to take the reins for a little while?" she asked.

"I'm fine."

If she'd been standing she would have stomped her foot. "Just *saying* you're fine doesn't make it so. There's nothing wrong with admitting you're sick."

"I told you, I don't get sick." The words were almost a growl and his tone would have been intimidating if it hadn't ended on a particularly nasty cough.

Besides, did he have any idea how absolutely ridiculous that assertion sounded? "I don't think that's something you have absolute control over. And anyway, that cough of yours seems to be contradicting your statement."

His only response was a tightening of his jaw and a quick flicking of the reins.

They rode along without speaking for a while. Finally she broke the silence again, trying for a less volatile subject. "How much longer until we get to this Cornerstone of yours?"

"It's not mine." He shot her a quick look, then softened his tone. "It's about another hour and a half." His lips quirked up in a self-mocking grin. "Why? Are you tired of the traveling or of the company?"

"Just curious." She lifted Patience onto her lap, looking for a bit of moral support. "But you know, maybe you should think about spending the night there yourself, especially if it's still raining when we arrive. The sooner you get dried out in front of a fire the better."

His irritation flared again. "Hang it all, will you *please* stop acting as if I'm about to keel over dead? For the last time, it's just a cough. And since Hawk's Creek is only another thirty minutes past Cornerstone, I'd just as soon dry out in front of my own fire in my own house."

But Ruby focused on the pallor of his complexion and the unhealthy glitter of his eyes rather than his tone. If she wasn't mistaken, he was running a fever. By the time they reached Cornerstone, would he even be capable of going on alone? If not, would she be able to stop him? "Is there a doctor in Cornerstone?"

He shot her another of those glowers and she held up a hand. "I'm just making conversation."

"No," he answered. "About the only thing you'll find in Cornerstone is a church, a schoolhouse and a general store."

That wasn't a town, it was a stopover. "So where do folks around there go for treatment when they get sick?"

He shrugged. "Most families take care of their own when they can. There are doctors in Tyler if it's something really serious." He shifted in his seat, grimacing. "Inez is pretty good with treating folks at Hawk's Creek when we're ailing or get injured."

That comment sent her thoughts down a different rabbit trail. "How many folks live at your ranch?"

He seemed happier with this topic. "Me and Inez, of course. Then there's Red, the ranch foreman, Manny who helps out around the place and three other hands who stay on year-round. We hire on more help during the busier times."

It must be a bigger place than she'd thought. "Is cattle all you deal with?"

"We raise horses, too, but mostly for our own use. There's a small peach orchard and we grow most of our own feed—hay, oats, corn, wheat. But yes, cattle is our main focus."

Ruby absently stroked Patience's head. "And you enjoy it? Raising cattle, I mean."

"Yep. Would have looked for other work years ago if I didn't."

"So what is it that you like about it?"

"Just about everything." He gave her a quick look. "Watching the new calves being born and growing into healthy livestock. Seeing the land green up every spring and burst out with new life. The sweet way the hay and the grain smell when it's harvested. Riding across acre after acre of Hawk's Creek and knowing my father and grandfather rode those same paths before me. And that, God willing, my own children will ride them, too, someday."

She watched Griff's face as he talked, enthralled by the passion she saw there. He truly did love that place and the way of life it provided.

Fifteen minutes later the rain had progressed from a light drizzle to a steady shower. Even worse, a gusty wind had kicked up and was periodically spitting the cold rain in their faces. Griff was visibly shivering. She tucked the lap robe more snugly around him without asking, then offered to take the reins "for a while." It was telling that he didn't put up an argument on either front.

Another ten minutes and she was getting seriously concerned that he wouldn't be upright much longer.

"I think a change of plans might be in order," he said after another spasm of coughs.

"What did you have in mind?"

"If you have no objections, I think it would be better to take you on to Hawk's Creek with me rather than drop you off at Cornerstone."

She felt a little spurt of pleasure at the thought that he wanted to show her his homeplace. "I'd certainly enjoy seeing this wonderful ranch you've been telling me about."

"Of course. But more importantly, if we bypass Cornerstone altogether, there's a shortcut we can take. The road's not quite as good, but it'll cut about thirty minutes off of the trip."

Oh. He was being practical, not neighborly. "Then that's definitely the way to go. I won't get a lick of sleep tonight unless I know you made it safely there."

He managed a smile. "Wouldn't want to be responsible for you not getting a good night's rest." Then he sobered. "Keep an eye out for a large oak with one side sheared off by lightning. A little ways past that you'll see a road branch off to your right. That's our shortcut—it'll take you right to Hawk's Creek."

A few minutes later she spied the milestone he'd mentioned. "There's the scorched tree."

He straightened and focused where she pointed. "That's it. The road we want is just up ahead. See it?"

She nodded and in short order had the buggy moving along the shortcut. It wasn't quite as wide or smooth as the road they'd been traveling before, but it was passable, even in this weather.

"Another thirty minutes and we'll be there," he said thickly.

Would he be able to stay upright that long? "Is there any place we can stop along the way? Any neighbors we'll pass before we get to your place?"

"No." Another bout of coughs. "The first part borders the back side of the Davis place—the house and barn are a ways off in the other direction. The rest of the road borders Hawk's Creek pasture land. The closest shelter is, in fact, my house at Hawk's Creek."

Not the answer she'd hoped for. "All right, then tell me what I'm looking for."

He slumped then roused himself. "You won't be able to miss it." He was mumbling now. "There's an ironwork arch over the entryway with the ranch's name on it."

Sounded easy enough.

Now if she could just keep him from falling out of the buggy until she got them there.

When he swayed again she decided drastic measures were in order. "Scoot over here."

"What?" He seemed to be having trouble focusing on her.

"I said scoot over here. I want you to lean against me to help brace yourself."

"I don't think—"

The man was impossible! "Listen, I've put up with your stubbornness and fool pride up until now but I'm cold and wet and tired and I don't have time for that anymore. And neither do you."

His head came up and he blinked at her.

"You've been none too steady these past few minutes," she continued, ignoring his reaction. "It's obvious you won't stay upright on your own power much longer."

"I can manage until we get there," he said stiffly.

"I doubt it." She wasn't going to sugarcoat this for him. "Even if tumbling out doesn't break your neck, there's no way I could get you back up here once you hit the ground." She took her eyes off the road long enough to glare at him. "Now do as I say and get over here."

He held his position a few moments longer, then slowly slid over until their shoulders touched. He was so stiff she feared he would snap in half at the least bit of jarring.

Did he find contact with her so distasteful? Regardless of his reasons, from the looks of him he wouldn't be able to keep that rigid stance up for long.

"Relax." She tried to keep her tone firm but sympathetic. "Lean against me if you need to. The best thing you can do right now is to focus your energy on staying conscious."

He nodded but his stiffness remained.

In a matter of minutes, however, he was starting to slump again. His head came down on her shoulder and she could feel the heat of his forehead through her clothing. He definitely had a fever.

She had to do what she could to keep him awake. "Griff, I need you to talk to me."

"What? I—" His head came up again. "Sorry."

"No, that's okay. Lean on me if it helps, just stay awake. Why don't you tell me about Inez? You say she's been at Hawk's Creek since before you were born. Was *she* born there?"

"No." His shoulders fluttered in a shiver. "But she was very young when my grandfather hired her." He coughed again and she winced at the painfully raspy sound of it.

But she had to keep him talking. "So he hired her as his housekeeper and she's been there ever since. Is that it?"

"Almost. He hired her to help take care of my grandmother when she got real sick. The way I hear it, she took over the cooking on her own. Grandmother never did get well again and…once she passed…Inez stayed on to…to run the household."

He was mumbling now and she only caught snatches of the rest of his answer. "…wish…woman like that…keeps her word…someone to stay." He slumped against her again and Ruby reflexively put an arm around his shoulder to hold him upright. No time to think about what his words might mean.

Lord, I need You to help me. Keep Griff from slipping down for just a bit longer. Guide me so I don't miss the gate to the ranch. And please don't let anything get in my path. I know that's asking a lot, but I also know there isn't anything You can't do.

Ruby repeated that prayer several times over the next fifteen minutes as the rain came down harder and the wind grew gustier. Her arm and shoulder ached almost unbearably from the effort to hold on to Griff, but she didn't dare take her arm from around his shoulder for fear he would slip down. Her teeth chattered from the cold as the rain blew into the buggy and soaked them both. Griff spoke periodically and tried pulling away from her, but his words were indistinct and his efforts were weak.

Twice she almost pulled the buggy over to wait out the storm, but she knew she had to get her companion to a warm, dry place as soon as possible. And if his instructions had been correct they had to be getting close.

"Hold on, please, we must be almost there. You're going to be able to warm yourself by your own fire and sleep in your own bed tonight after all, just like you wanted. I promise."

Her only answer was another spasm of coughs.

Please God, don't let me break that promise.

Griff felt disoriented. Time seemed to be jumping around. This was the third time he'd opened his eyes with no recollection of having closed them. And the weather kept getting worse each time with no transition from what it had been before. The rain was really coming down now and he felt chilled to the bone. Something was constricting him, keeping him from moving. That wouldn't do. He tried pushing free but it was no good...

He roused what seemed a few minutes later to the feel of a soft shoulder cushioning his head and an arm around his shoulder. Is that what had held him earlier? He couldn't remember.

His companion was talking under her breath—it sounded like a strange combination of prayer and an exhortation to him to not fall out of the buggy. A sudden catch in her voice, as if on a sob, set off alarm bells in his head. What was the matter? Had something happened to her? He should reassure her. After all, it was his job as her escort keep her safe. And he'd do that just as soon...

Voices. So many voices. They were coming at him from everywhere. But the words were garbled, urgent. He even heard that scraggly cat of hers complaining loudly. Where was Ruby? Then there were hands, lots of hands, grabbing at him, tugging on him, carrying him. The jostling made the pounding in his head worse. But he couldn't let that stop him.

Where was Ruby? Were these hands after her, too? Was she safe? He had to make certain. She'd counted on him.

He struggled, but there were too many of them and they were too strong. Or maybe he was too weak. How could he be so hot and so cold at the same time? It was as if his head was disconnected from the rest of his body.

He called out Ruby's name. She answered, but her voice was so distant. Was she still crying? He couldn't tell.

Then the blackness swallowed him completely.

Chapter Five

Griff bobbed in and out of consciousness for a while, like a cork on choppy water. He wanted to sleep, to find relief from the pounding and the burning and the steel band wrapped around his chest, but the nagging feeling that there was something important he needed to do kept tugging him back to the surface again.

Ruby. She'd been crying. He had to make certain she was okay. But, no matter how hard he tried, his eyelids and arms wouldn't cooperate and down he'd go again.

Finally he drifted up and this time the surface was cool and quiet, and the bands on his chest had loosened. This time he could actually open his eyes, though it was dark here, wherever *here* was.

Then the memories slammed into him—nightmare images of voices and hands, fire and chills, a yowling cat and...

And Ruby! He was supposed to provide her with safe escort. Was she okay? Had she—

"Well, hello there."

She stood over him, a shadowy form in the dimness. Her voice was thick, as if she'd been asleep. Or weeping.

Had something happened to her? If only he could see her more clearly. "Are you okay?"

"I'm fine."

"But you were crying."

"I'm all better now."

"Good." Griff settled back down. There was something heavy on his chest. From the pungent odor, he figured it was one of Inez's poultices. The thing itched and smelled—it had to come off. He just needed a minute to gather his thoughts and his strength…

Griff barely blinked yet sunshine was now streaming into the room.

Ruby appeared at his bedside and smiled down at him. "Good, you're awake again. You had us mighty worried. Now, you just rest easy while I let Inez know you're awake."

"Wait."

She paused and came closer. Close enough that he could see the tired circles under her eyes.

"Is something wrong?" she asked. "Do you need me to get you anything?"

"No. I—" He tried to gather his scattered thoughts. "What day is it?"

"Tuesday."

He frowned. "Tuesday? But that means I lost two and a half days."

Her dimples appeared. "You didn't lose them—you spent both of them right here."

Whatever else had happened, she hadn't lost her sense of humor. "I guess I owe you a big thank-you for getting me home the way you did."

She waved him off. "I'm just glad that things turned out okay. And Inez has been treating me very well since I arrived, so there's no need for any other thanks." She turned to the door. "Speaking of Inez, I promised I'd let her know the second you woke up. She's been beside herself worrying about you."

After she'd left the room, Griff looked around. This wasn't his bedchamber. In fact, it wasn't a bedchamber at all—it was his mother's sitting room, a room that was rarely used anymore. Someone had pushed the furniture to one side and a bed had been set up near the fireplace.

He winced as he shifted, trying for a more comfortable position. His chest muscles were sore as all get out. And why in the world was his left foot tender? It seemed he'd been a lot sicker—and a lot more out of it—than he'd thought. Pretty lowering to realize he'd put Ruby in a position to have to deal with his troubles.

His sister, Sadie, had always said his stubbornness was going to be the death of him—seems he'd nearly proved her right. Why in the world hadn't he sought out a dry place to wait out the bad weather?

Then again, whatever ailment had laid him low might have overtaken him regardless of the weather. So pushing to get back to Hawk's Creek and Inez's ministrations just might have been the best plan after all.

Feeling better about his decisions, Griff took stock of himself and his surroundings.

The poultice was gone—if it had ever been there in the first place. He wasn't sure how much of the past few days was memory and how much delirium.

He stared up at the ceiling. He had only hazy memories of what had transpired once they'd turned onto that shortcut—just the jostle of the ride, the pounding of his head and his losing battle to stay conscious.

Wait a minute, there was something else—a scolding she'd given him and the feel of her arm holding him snug against her side. Had that really happened? The memory felt real enough. But how could a girl like Ruby have managed his practically dead weight while driving the buggy, especially in that weather?

He still had trouble believing she'd gotten him home when he'd been too sick to get himself here. For a wide-eyed dreamer, she'd sure proven herself resourceful in a pinch. Perhaps the good Lord had actually been looking out for *his* well-being more than Ruby's when He'd put her in his path.

And it was curious that she was still here. Why hadn't she gone on to Tyler? Had she been worried about him? Or was she getting cold feet about her plans for a new life?

Inez bustled in, interrupting his thoughts. "Now ain't you a sight for sore eyes." Her voice was gruff and she looked at him as if he'd been at death's doorstep. "I was beginning to wonder if you were gonna sleep straight through to Christmas."

He gave her a teasing smile. "Now you know you can't get shed of me that easy. I'm too tough to stay down long."

"Too ornery is more like it." She placed a hand on his forehead. "Fever seems to be all gone. How are you feeling?"

His throat and chest ached, but the pounding in his head was gone and his thinking was clear. "I won't be roping any steers or running any races today, but compared to how I felt Saturday, I'm fine."

She harrumphed. "I think *fine* is a bit optimistic, what with you lying there looking wrung out as wet laundry, but I'm glad to hear you're better."

Griff pushed himself up to a semi-sitting position. "Wet laundry? I'll have you know I'm feeling stronger by the minute." He patted his stomach. "All I need is to get some of your hearty meals in me and I'll be right as rain."

She reached behind him and plumped the pillows. "Don't be expecting steak and potatoes just yet. It's broths and soups for you until you're a bit stronger."

"Yes, ma'am." He smiled innocently up at her. "But it seems to me I'd get stronger a lot quicker with heartier nourishment."

Inez placed her hands on her hips, just as he'd known she would. "Since I'm doing the cooking and the doctorin', with Ruby's help, I'll decide what you need."

What all had Ruby's help consisted of? "I appreciate you looking out for Miss Tuggle the past few days. I hope having her around hasn't added to your work."

"Land sakes, no. In fact, she's been a big help. Spelling me in watching over you, making herself useful in the kitchen."

Ruby had watched over him? For some reason that made him decidedly uncomfortable. "I hope I wasn't too much trouble for you ladies the past few days."

"We managed."

That wasn't exactly an answer. But before he could dig deeper, she changed the subject. "How's your foot feeling?"

"A mite sore, but not anything I can't deal with. I don't recall hurting it though."

"We had some trouble getting you out of the buggy when y'all arrived. Truth to tell, you were delirious with the fever and fought us like a rabid wolf. I'm afraid your foot got banged up in the process. But don't go blaming Red and the guys—it was an accident."

"Seems I'd better be doing more apologizing than blaming." He stiffened at a sudden thought. "I didn't hurt anyone, did I?"

She gave him a sympathetic smile. "I'm afraid you left a few bruises here and there, but nothing worse."

What about Ruby? Was that why he remembered her crying? Please, God, don't let him have hurt her. "I didn't hurt Ruby, did—"

She looked up quickly. "Mercy, no. No worries there. In fact, you seemed to think you were protecting her from goodness only knows what."

Griff released a breath he hadn't realized he'd been holding. At least he didn't have that on his conscience.

"She's quite a girl, isn't she?" Inez added.

Griff nodded. He was beginning to see that himself.

"The good Lord was sure looking after you when He arranged for you two to travel together," she said, echoing his earlier thoughts. "I don't like to think what might have happened if you'd taken ill alone on that road. That girl likely saved your life."

Before Griff could question her further, Ruby stepped through the open doorway, carrying a tray of food. Her cat was right at her heels.

"Here we go," she said cheerily. "Inez's marvelous cooking ought to help fix you right up."

"Mmm-mmm. That sure does smell good." He watched her closely, looking for some sign that she might be leery of him. "What is it?"

"Beef and vegetable broth." Inez answered for her, patting his coverlet before she stepped back. "I expect you to eat it all up."

"Don't worry. I feel like I could eat a whole steer, hooves, horns and all."

"Well, for today you'll just have to settle for the broth. If you behave yourself and rest like you're supposed to, I just might leave some meat and vegetables in it tomorrow."

Ruby watched the interaction between Inez and Griff with surprise and a touch of longing. Griff didn't balk at Inez's solicitousness the way he had with her. The two obviously cared for each other, as if the housekeeper were indeed part of his family, just as he'd claimed. How would it be to have someone in her own life who cared as much for her? The closest emotion she'd felt from her surrogate parents was care born of obligation.

Inez turned to Ruby, pulling her out of her thoughts. "If you don't mind, would you stay here and help Griff with his meal? I want to let Red and the others know that he's feeling better this morning."

"Oh, but I can do that if you—"

Inez waved away her offer. "No, no. I need to talk to Red about something else anyway." She glanced at Griff, then back to Ruby. "I can count on you to stay with him until he finishes every bit of that soup, can't I?"

"Of course."

Ruby faced Griff, feeling suddenly uncertain. She'd spent the past few days taking shifts watching over him in this very room, but an unconscious Griff Lassiter was very different from this alert, watchful man. Suddenly, the memory of holding him tight against her side in the pouring rain during the last twenty minutes of that awful drive was all she could think about.

Pasting a bright smile on her face that she hoped would mask her nervousness, she lifted the tray slightly. "Where would you like me to place this?"

He patted the coverlet in front of him. "Just set it here on my lap and I'll take it from there."

She did as he asked, helped him tuck a napkin

under his chin, then pulled a chair up closer to his bedside. “Do you need any help with that?”

“I can manage.”

She noticed his hand shook slightly as he ladled up a spoonful, but didn’t comment on it. She knew him well enough now to understand he wouldn’t appreciate her pointing out such a weakness.

Instead, she kept him company the best way she knew how—chatting. “I had a bowl myself earlier. Inez is quite a cook.” She reached down to stroke her cat’s head. “I can see why you spoke so highly of her. And I don’t mean just for her cooking ability. She’s nice.” Even knowing Inez would likely have offered the same to anyone, it had warmed Ruby to have someone offer genuine neighborliness, not a handout born of a sense of duty.

Griff scooped up another spoonful. “Couldn’t run this place without her.” He nodded Ruby’s way. “She had good things to say about you, too. I understand you’ve been lending a hand around here the past few days.”

Inez had spoken well of her? Ruby’s smile stretched wider. “I like to keep busy. And it was the least I could do in return for Patience and my room and board.”

He frowned at that. “We don’t usually ask our guests to work off their room and board.”

“Oh, I didn’t mean to imply Inez *asked* me to work. I pestered her to let me help.”

He took another sip of his soup, but he kept his gaze on her and she was having trouble interpreting his expression.

"Sorry if my condition caused you to delay your trip to Tyler," he said finally.

Actually, she hadn't even thought about Tyler since she'd arrived here. "Oh, I don't mind. It wasn't as if I had to be there on a specific date."

"True." Another pause to eat, then, "The last part of that trip home is hazy for me. Care to fill in the blanks?"

She tried to keep her expression even as she remembered just how tense, how frightening the final leg of that ride had been. There were moments when she'd thought for sure he'd slide right off the carriage seat.

But she didn't need to burden him with all of that. Instead she gave him a smile. "You stayed coherent long enough to point out the road I needed to take to get us on the shortcut. Then I just followed it until I found the wrought-iron arch with Hawk's Creek Ranch spelled out." Of course the rain had been coming down so hard at that point she'd had trouble making it out. She pushed that thought aside. "You gave good directions. When I pulled up at the house Inez and some of the ranch hands were waiting on me. Apparently someone spotted the buggy coming up the drive. Then they got you in the house and Inez took over." Ruby grinned. "She's very good at taking charge."

"That she is." He grimaced. "I guess I wasn't much good as an escort after all. Sorry if I gave you a scare."

That was putting it mildly. "I'm just happy it all

turned out okay." She sat up straighter. "And you'll be pleased to know that yesterday, when I mentioned the bull we'd left behind at the Callums's place, Red immediately sent someone out to fetch it."

Griff nodded. "Red is a good man."

"And everyone's been just as nice as could be to me. Of course, once they had you settled in, I *did* have to do some explaining as to how I came to be riding with you."

He grinned. "I imagine you did."

She'd been amazed that Inez and the others had heard her out and then took her in as if she were an old family friend instead of a stranger. She wasn't used to receiving such an unconditional welcome.

"I hope you won't think me awful for saying this," she said impulsively, "but if you *had* to get sick, I'm glad I was with you when you did."

He raised a brow and she felt her face warm. That hadn't come out quite right. "I mean, it gave me a chance to spend a little time here at Hawk's Creek. And it's every bit as nice as you described it. I can see why you're so proud of it."

He nodded, obviously pleased with her comment. "There's no other place on earth like Hawk's Creek." Then he cocked his head to one side. "Have you seen much of the ranch itself?"

She shook her head. "I've stayed close to the house." To be more specific, she'd been staying pretty close to the sickroom—sightseeing had been the furthest thing from her mind the past few days. "But I like what I've seen of it."

"If you've stayed close to the house, then you haven't really seen Hawk's Creek. I'll have to take you for a ride across the place when I get my strength back."

"Oh, I'd enjoy that. But it may be a few days before you're up to a ride."

"You said yourself you didn't have to be in Tyler by any particular date. Or are you in hurry to get there after all?"

"Well, I..." Ruby paused. Was she? She'd lingered here because she wanted to satisfy herself that he was going to be okay. It appeared that was no longer an issue so there wasn't anything to keep her here now.

But, truly, her main goal hadn't been to get to Tyler so much as to get out of Cleebit Springs. And she'd accomplished that. The rest of her fresh start could wait a bit longer.

Ruby smiled. "No, I suppose not. Establishing a new home for myself by Thanksgiving is my only goal. So, as long as I reach Tyler by then, I'm happy to stay here for a few days."

"Then consider yourself our guest for the time being." He pointed his spoon her way. "And none of this 'earning your keep' business, either."

She had no intention of sitting idle for the next few days, but there was no point in getting him agitated by saying so. "Thank you kindly for the invitation." Then she stood. "Now, it looks like you've scraped the bottom of that bowl, so I'll take your tray and let you get a little more rest."

"Rest." He snorted. "I've been *resting* since I got here." But even as he spoke she saw him stifle a yawn.

"You've been fighting a fever since then, which is not at all the same thing as resting. You need to get some real rest if you want to get your strength back. And since you now owe me a tour of the place, I insist." She placed the tray on the chair and reached for the pillows behind his back. "Now, slide down and try to sleep." Not that she figured it would take much trying. He'd probably be asleep before she and Patience made it to the kitchen.

Griff watched her disappear into the hallway, then settled deeper under the covers. He wasn't sure exactly why he'd invited her to stay—gratitude, he supposed. After all, she'd gone through a lot to get him here, and Inez had mentioned how much help she'd been since her arrival.

Ruby Tuggle had to be one of the most deliberately agreeable people he'd ever met. Always trying to please the people she was with, always apologizing when she thought she'd failed, always looking for the bright side of bad situations. Nobody could be that pleasant all the time. What was her story?

He shifted, trying to get more comfortable. Inez hadn't been far off when she pronounced him to be as useful as damp laundry—definitely unfamiliar territory for him. He hadn't been lying when he told Ruby he never got sick. It was embarrassing to realize he'd been laid so low while she was supposed to be in his charge. Seems she'd managed okay on her own, though. She was either very lucky or more resourceful than he'd given her credit for.

Well, he'd make it up to her once he got his strength back. And then he'd personally see her settled safely in Tyler, and by Thanksgiving if that's what she really wanted. He still didn't understand her reasoning, but if life there was her goal, then he aimed to see she got off on the right foot. Perhaps he should even go so far as to look in on her from time to time. Whenever he was already in Tyler on business, of course. After all, with what she'd done for him, he owed her that much.

This was about paying his debts, he told himself. Nothing more.

Chapter Six

Inez looked up from peeling carrots as Ruby entered the kitchen. "So how's our patient doing?"

"He ate all of his soup and now he's resting." Ruby unloaded the tray of dishes into the sink. "He claimed to be all rested up, but from the looks of him he'll fall back asleep in no time."

Inez gave her a surprised look. "You got him to settle back down, just like that?"

Had she done something wrong? "I thought sleep was what he needed right now."

"Oh, it is. But that doesn't mean Griff will be sensible about it." She shook her head. "I guess you haven't been around him long enough to understand just how stubborn that boy can be."

Ruby smiled. It seemed strange for anyone to call such an impressive man "that boy." "Actually, I did get a taste of that side of him during our ride." She cleared her throat. "I hope you won't mind having me and Patience around a little longer. Mr. Lassiter invited me to stick around for a few more days."

Inez gave her another of those surprised looks, then wiped her hands on her apron. "Good for him. It's been nice to have another female around the place and I'm right pleased to know you'll be staying awhile longer." She moved to the stove with her peeled carrots. "And now that we know he's on the mend, you and I can relax a bit and get to know each other better."

"I'd like that." Feeling as if her world was finally coming to rights after so many years, Ruby began washing the dishes. "But I aim to help out while I'm here. You just let me know what needs doing."

The next time Griff opened his eyes, there were lamps lit and the corners of the room were in shadow. Evening, then—but was it the same day? He turned toward the sound of movement and found Inez rather than Ruby near his bedside.

Surely that was curiosity and not disappointment he felt?

"I thought you might be ready for some supper." Inez nodded toward a tray on the bedside table.

"You thought right." Griff pulled himself into a sitting position. "How long did I sleep this time?"

"About six hours."

At least he hadn't lost another day.

Inez started fussing with the pillows at his back. "You'll be pleased to know there's a bit of substance in your bowl this time. You can thank Ruby for that.

I was going to give you another bowl of plain broth but she seems to think you're ready for something a little heartier than that."

Another point in the girl's favor. "Speaking of Miss Tuggle," he said casually, "how is she this evening?"

"I made her sit down a few minutes ago and eat her own supper. That girl has more energy than a wild mustang."

He frowned. "I told her she's a guest here, that she doesn't need to earn her keep."

Inez shrugged as she placed the tray on his lap. "I told her the same thing but she claims she likes to keep busy. Besides, I enjoy the company." She took a seat beside him and pulled some mending from her sewing bag.

Had that been in here earlier? He couldn't remember.

"She tells me you invited her to stay on for a spell."

Griff resisted the urge to squirm under his housekeeper's probing gaze. "The fool girl is planning to move to Tyler all on her own," he explained, "and she doesn't know a soul there. I figure I owe it to her to make sure she gets settled in okay." He swirled the spoon through his soup. "To do that, I need to keep her here long enough for me to get back on my feet so I can take her there myself."

"I see. That makes sense." Inez kept her eyes focused on her sewing. "She also tells me you climbed a tree to rescue that cat of hers."

For some reason Griff felt a touch of heat climb into his cheeks. Was his fever returning? "I didn't have much choice." Why did he feel so defensive? "Ruby wasn't going to leave without her pet and I didn't have all day to hang around waiting for that stubborn critter to come down on its own."

"Well, whatever the circumstances, she's convinced you're quite the hero."

Hero! Of all the foolish, schoolgirl notions. "I'm nobody's hero." Especially after the way he'd fallen apart during the last leg of their trip. Still, there was something about the notion that she'd actually said that…

He caught Inez looking at him with a twinkle in her eye and decided to change the subject. "I guess I was a sorry sight by the time she got me here."

"Mercy me, yes. Wet as a drowned cub and half out of your mind from the fever. I don't know how that girl managed to keep hold of you and handle that buggy in the pouring rain."

Griff paused with the spoon halfway to his mouth. Keep hold of him? So he hadn't imagined that arm around his shoulder. "Seems there was more to this little adventure than I remember," he said slowly. "Want to fill me in?"

Inez didn't look up from her stitches. "Well, the rain had turned from a drizzle to a downpour and it was miserable cold. Not a fit day for man nor beast. We all figured you'd taken shelter somewhere like any *sensible* person would have." The look she gave him was that of a schoolmarm confronting a truant.

Griff felt compelled to explain himself. "Can you blame me for wanting to get back here as soon as possible? After all, no one can take care of me like you can."

"Don't go trying to smooth-talk me, Griff Lassiter. I know your tricks." But her expression had softened considerably.

"Anyway," she continued, "we weren't really looking for you to arrive until the next day. Thank goodness, or I should say thank the good Lord, Red just happened to be looking out from the barn when he spied the wagon coming up the drive. Didn't recognize it, of course, but he figured it had to be something important to bring anyone out in that weather, so he ran out to meet it. Good thing he did, too. Poor Ruby was just about at the end of her stamina what with trying to handle the reins and hold on to you at the same time."

Inez's hands stilled. "It's a wonder that poor child was able to see the gate, much less turn the horse onto the drive."

Griff had given up all pretense of eating. "I didn't realize—"

"Of course you didn't. Thing is, you may have been bad sick, but that didn't keep you from fighting off everyone who tried to help you, mumbling incoherent protests. Red and the boys had a terrible time getting you inside."

Griff groaned. Sounds like he'd made quite a spectacle of himself.

"Poor Ruby was soaked to the skin and her lips were practically blue with cold. I was worried for a while that I would have two patients on my hands."

"She seems okay now." No thanks to him.

"Oh, she's fine. That girl is a lot stronger than she looks." Inez patted his arm. "But there's no reason for you to be too hard on yourself. You were sick and that likely clouded your thinking a mite."

Was that supposed to make him feel better?

"Besides," she continued, picking her sewing back up, "Ruby doesn't blame you. And it all turned out well enough in the end."

Ruby might not blame him but that didn't mean he was blameless. He'd have to find a way to make it up to her.

Ruby looked up guiltily as Inez entered the kitchen. She'd been down on the floor, slipping Patience a sliver of meat from her bowl of stew. But either Inez didn't notice, or didn't care.

"So was he awake?" Ruby asked as she straightened.

"Yep. And he ate every last bit of his supper. At this rate he'll be up and about in no time."

Inez sounded in remarkably good spirits. Griff must be doing well indeed. Would it seem impertinent if she checked in on him herself?

"The only fly in the ointment," Inez continued, "is that he's feeling restless now. I'm worried he'll try to get up before he should."

"Is there something I can do to help? Would you like me to sit with him for a while?"

Inez gave her a bright smile. "That's a wonderful

idea. Actually, why don't you see if there's something more active you can do to keep him occupied?"

That sounded interesting. "Such as?"

"Oh, I don't know. Perhaps a game of checkers, or there's a flute in the study if you play, or maybe get a book and read—"

Ruby's pulse quickened. "Do you have many books here?"

"A fair number." She must have noticed Ruby's excitement because she gave a help-yourself-to-them smile. "They're in the study, which is right across the hall from the room where we put Griff. You're welcome to borrow any of them any time while you're here."

"Thank you. That sounds lovely."

"For now, why don't you see if you can find a book you might both enjoy?"

"Do you know what kind of books he likes?" Ruby was already headed toward the hall.

"As far as I can tell, when it comes to books he likes just about everything."

A man after her own heart. Ruby glanced back at her pet. "Coming, Patience?"

But Inez waved her on. "Leave the cat, she'll keep me company. And I'll pour her up a saucer of buttermilk to keep her happy."

A few moments later, Ruby entered the study, then stopped in her tracks. Being in the possession of her father's three books had made her an exception of sorts in Cleebit Springs. Sure, there were newspapers and catalogs, but other than Bibles and schoolbooks, few of the families had access to very many actual bound books.

But here, in this room, were literally hundreds of volumes. Two entire walls were lined with tall bookcases and all of them were laden with volume upon volume of various sizes and colors. She'd never seen so many books in her entire life. Ruby approached them almost reverently, running her fingers across the spines, reading the titles, imagining the hours she could spend here blissfully lost in such a wealth of information and imagination.

She wasn't sure how long she stood lost in the grandness of it all, until she finally remembered the mission Inez had set her on. She was supposed to be selecting something appropriate to read to Griff.

A few minutes later she hesitated at his doorway. What if he had already fallen asleep? Or worse yet, what if he wished to be alone and saw her visit as an intrusion? What was that he'd said that day on the road—*sometimes a fellow just liked to hear his own thoughts for a while.*

Then again, if he was lying there bored, he might be tempted to get up, and that would never do. She squared her shoulders and gave the door a light tap.

She received an immediate "Come in" reply. Pulling her shoulders back, she tried to decide if she was more nervous or excited by the prospect of visiting with him again.

And decided that it was perhaps a bit of both.

Chapter Seven

When Griff saw it was Ruby at the door, his spirits lifted. "Well, hello. Come to check on the invalid?" he asked as he pushed himself up to a sitting position. The spurt of pleasure he felt at seeing her was due to his need to repay her for her help in getting him home, of course.

She returned his smile. "You're looking less like an invalid by the minute."

Pleased that she'd noticed, he nodded. "Thanks. Regardless of what Inez has to say on the matter, it's not really necessary to keep me bed-bound like this."

"She's only looking out for your best interests."

"I know. That's why I'm humoring her today. But tomorrow I'm getting out of this bed and out of this room, no matter how much she tries to mollycoddle me."

"Do you really think that's wise? You're not—"

"I didn't say I was going to ride out to the back

forty. I just want to move around and get a change of scenery."

Ruby held up her hands, palms outward. "No need to get all testy. It's not me you'll need to convince."

"And you don't think I can convince Inez?"

She dropped her hands. "I'll let the two of you battle that out without me." The she grinned. "And don't ask me who I'd favor to come out on top."

He pretended indignation. "I'll grant that Inez can be a formidable opponent. But don't rule me out just yet."

"Oh, I would never *completely* rule you out."

He glanced at the object in her hands. "What do you have there?"

"A book." Then she quickly added, "Inez told me I could borrow it."

"Of course. I was just curious as to which book it was."

"*A Connecticut Yankee in King Arthur's Court.* It's by Mr. Mark Twain. Have you read it?"

"I have." He noticed the way her expression fell.

"Oh. I thought I would read it to you for a while, but if you've already—"

"I'd rather just talk, if you don't mind. Maybe you could read it yourself later and we could compare notes on what we each thought of it."

"All right." She set the book on the side table somewhat wistfully and took a seat. "What would you like to talk about?"

He grabbed the first topic that came to mind. "You enjoy reading?"

"Oh, yes. I own three books myself." Her pride changed to chagrin in an instant. "Of course, compared to what you have here, that must sound meager."

"Not at all. You have to understand, that library was collected by several family members over many, many years. I'm afraid I haven't added much to the collection myself."

"You're blessed to have access to so many volumes."

"I take it you didn't?"

"Other than Bibles, not many of the families in Cleebit Springs have books. But I didn't go entirely without. Mr. Barlowe, who owns the general store, used to get the newspaper from Shreveport and when I lived with his family he would let me read it occasionally. And Mrs. Samuels had a set of encyclopedias that I spent as much time with as I could when I lived with her family."

Sounded as if she'd moved around a lot growing up.

"The books I have were my father's," she continued. "One of them is another of Mr. Twain's books—*The Prince and the Pauper.*"

"That's one I haven't read yet. Did you enjoy it?"

"Very much." She brightened. "I'd be glad to loan it to you if you like."

"Why don't you tell me about it?"

"All right." She leaned forward and launched into an enthusiastic discussion of the high points of the story, complete with animated expressions and hand gestures. She seemed to be quite a storyteller in her own right.

Griff interposed questions and comments of his own, as much to keep her talking as for clarification. He was surprised at both her recall and the intelligent way she added asides about her own thoughts on the story.

When Inez stepped into the room, Griff glanced at the clock on the mantel and was surprised to find that nearly two hours had passed.

"Sounds like you two are passing the time enjoyably," Inez commented, "but I think maybe Griff should get some rest now. As should we all."

Ruby popped out of her chair, a guilty flush staining her cheeks. "Oh, I'm so sorry. I lost all track of time. I—"

"No need to apologize," Griff interrupted. Truth to tell he was annoyed at Inez's interruption. He wasn't some schoolboy to be given an early bedtime. "In fact, I was enjoying the story."

"That's all well and good," Inez replied, "but you're still my patient and I say it's time for you to rest."

"I'm not tired." He mentally winced at the petulance of his tone. It didn't help when he spied Ruby's unsuccessful attempt to swallow her grin.

"Well, Ruby and I have had a long day." Inez's tone was tart. "And neither of us got much sleep the past two nights."

A not-so-subtle reminder of the worry he'd caused them.

"Now, before we leave you to your rest," she said as she turned down the wick of the lamp, "would you like me to fix you one of my special teas to help you sleep?"

Griff shook his head and leaned back against the pillows. "No, thanks."

"Good." She made shooing motions for Ruby. "We'll leave you, then."

Griff frowned at her high-handedness, then shifted uncomfortably as his housekeeper shot him a look he couldn't quite interpret. Surely that wasn't amusement?

"Just a minute." Ruby moved back toward the bed and slipped the pillows out from behind his back. "Slide down and I'll straighten your covers."

"Tucking me in like a babe," Griff said gruffly. "You're as bad as Inez."

But even as he complained, Griff felt oddly warmed by the attention.

Ruby turned to Inez once they were in the hallway. "Honestly, I'm so sorry if I kept him up—"

Inez held up a hand. "No need to apologize. I'm sure your visit did him a world of good." Then she smiled and there was a definite twinkle in her eyes. "Most of my little performance was for his benefit. I wanted to make sure he wasn't in any position to argue with me."

Performance? Ruby gave her head a mental shake. The relationship between these two was more complex than she'd imagined. But there was genuine love on both ends, so she supposed that was what counted.

They paused at the foot of the stairs. Inez had her own set of rooms off the kitchen, away from the family area. She had placed Ruby in one of the guest rooms on the second floor.

"Now, I'm going to head off to my own bed," Inez said. "But if you want to stay up a bit longer, feel free."

They exchanged good-nights and Ruby slowly climbed the stairs, clutching the Mark Twain book to her chest. She'd read for a while before she turned down her lamp tonight. Then she could discuss the story with Griff tomorrow.

She'd certainly enjoyed their discussion tonight. It wasn't often someone sought out her opinion and then really listened to what she had to say. It had been a heady feeling.

Griff Lassiter was a man who was hard to put a label on—gruff and irritable one minute, considerate and gentle the next. But there was no doubting his compassion and integrity.

Strange that such a man had never married. Especially one who seemed so deeply rooted in his land and his family.

As she pushed open her bedroom door, Ruby told herself that that was really none of her business.

Still, the question lingered in her mind long after she'd turned down the lamp and pulled up the blanket.

Ruby looked up from turning the crank on the butter churn as Red entered the kitchen.

"Morning, ladies," he said as he removed his hat and stomped his boots on the rag rug at the threshold. "Another nasty day out there."

Inez wiped her hands on her apron as she moved to the cupboard. "Come on in and let me fix you a cup of coffee."

"No, thanks. I just had a cup at the bunkhouse. Manny tells me Griff wants me to fill him in on what's been going on around here since he left. I assume he's in his office."

Inez headed back to the stove. "Of course. You know Griff—he couldn't wait to get back to work."

Griff had prevailed this morning, getting up right after breakfast to bathe and shave. Afterward he'd headed straight for his office, where he'd been for the past twenty minutes. Ruby had only seen him briefly when she'd brought him a cup of coffee at Inez's request.

Red nodded to Ruby as he passed. "I noticed one of the traces on your buggy harness looked worn. I asked Frank to have a look at it. He'll make sure it's good as new before you need to take it out again."

Ruby was struck again by how thoughtful the folks here were. "Why, thank you. But y'all don't have to go to all that trouble."

"It's not any trouble to speak of. On a day like this there's not much else we can do anyway. And we can't have you breaking down when you're out and about on your own."

And before she could say more he had exited the room.

* * *

An hour later Ruby was happily ensconced in the study, curled up in an overstuffed chair, one hand holding an open book and the other hand resting on the cat slumbering in her lap. It felt almost decadent to relax this way in the middle of the day, but the guilty pleasure was one she could happily get used to.

Besides, Inez had run her out of the kitchen, ordering her to take some time for herself.

Patience's lifting of her head was Ruby's first sign that they were no longer alone. Looking toward the doorway, she saw Griff leaning there, watching her.

"Sorry," he said straightening. "Didn't mean to interrupt your reading."

How long had he been standing there? "Oh, that's okay." She uncurled her legs and put her feet on the floor.

"No need to get up on my account," he protested.

She settled back down. Making a quick mental note of the page number, she closed the book. "I hope you don't mind my being in here. Inez ran me out of the kitchen, and the weather's too dreary for me to go outside, so I thought I'd take advantage of your library and do a bit of reading while I still had the chance."

"Of course I don't mind. Spend as much time in here as you like." He moved to the chair across from her and she noticed the slight hitch in his gait. Apparently his foot still bothered him, but he was trying to hide it.

Patience sneezed, hopped off her lap and stalked from the room, head and tail equally high.

"I don't think that animal cares for me," Griff said.

She smiled at his dry tone. "Patience *is* a very discerning animal."

He stared at her a moment as if not certain if she'd been serious. Then he smiled. "So why did you name that pampered rat catcher Patience?"

She raised a brow. "What? You don't think it fits her?" Ruby laughed outright at his expression. "Actually, it's because patience is what was required to win her over."

"Ahh—now that I can believe. So, I take it she was a stray?"

"Uh-huh. I spotted her outside the boardinghouse shortly after I moved in there. Poor thing was skin and bones and had a hurt paw." But Ruby had recognized a kindred spirit beneath the tattered exterior.

"So you took her in."

"Not right away. She wasn't trusting enough for that. But after weeks of leaving food scraps for her and talking softly and being as nonthreatening as possible, she finally quit running away when she saw me. It was a lot longer before I could actually hold her." That had been such a sweet moment. Ruby could still remember that feeling of triumph and joy when she felt Patience begin to truly trust her.

"And now she's your pet."

Ruby grinned. "I don't know if I'd go that far—

Patience is much too independent for that. I guess you could say we have an understanding of sorts."

He shook his head. "Seems like a whole lot of trouble for a snooty, scruffy feline."

"You know what they say—appearances can be deceiving. Sometimes it's worth looking closer to see what's inside."

He gave her a strange look at that. But rather than comment, he changed the subject. "What's that you're reading?"

"It's the Mark Twain book I brought to your room last night. I'm really enjoying it."

"So are you going to focus only on Mr. Twain's work, or do you plan to try some other writers while you're here?"

She glanced at the shelves wistfully, wishing she had time to read each and every volume. "I'll admit I was overwhelmed by the bumper crop of choices and just went for the familiar."

He smiled. "Bumper crop, is it?" He moved toward the bookshelves. "Why don't I make some recommendations, if you'll allow me?"

"Oh, I'd appreciate that."

She followed him to the bookshelves where he started pulling books and handing them to her.

"The Twain books are all on this shelf—help yourself to any of them you're interested in. Now these over here are some of my personal favorites."

She read the titles as he handed them to her: *Swiss Family Robinson, The Count of Monte Cristo, A Tale of Two Cities, Around the World in Eighty Days,*

Castle Nowhere: Lake-Country Sketches, Twice-Told Tales.

He moved to another bookcase. "These are some of my sister's favorites." He handed her copies of *Pride and Prejudice, Little Women, Sonnets from the Portuguese, Alice's Adventures in Wonderland* and *Black Beauty.*

Then he turned and focused back on her, and the towering stack of books in her arms. "Oh, sorry. Here let me take those." He retrieved them from her and set them on a nearby table.

Ruby stared at the literary feast he'd selected for her. "My goodness, that's quite a pile of books. There's no way I can read all of them while I'm here." Unless she stayed longer than a day or two. Not that she wanted to extend her stay. She was ready to get on with her new life.

He shrugged. "What you don't finish you can take with you when you leave for Tyler. I can get them back from you when you're done with them."

So he expected to see her even after she moved? That thought lightened her mood considerably. It would be nice to have at least one friend in her life. "That's mighty generous. Thank you."

"It's the least I can do. After all, you practically saved my life."

Ruby went very still as the little bubble of joy inside her burst. He was being nice because he thought he *owed* her. Not because he actually wanted to befriend her. Truth was, she'd probably never have seen him again if she hadn't had to help him get home. Was that also the same reason Inez and Red and all the rest of them were being so nice?

Of course it was. She'd been silly to read anything else into their friendliness.

Something of what she was feeling must have shown on her face because he was looking at her with a puzzled expression. She pulled herself together and offered a big smile. "Now, I think I've lollygagged in here long enough. I should go and see if Inez needs any help."

"Inez will be just fine. She likes having her kitchen to herself." He moved to a table near the window where an inlaid checkerboard was displayed. "How about a game of checkers?"

She needed to find a quiet place to gather her thoughts, to start laying plans to leave. "I don't think—"

"You do know how to play, don't you?"

The challenge in his tone snagged her attention. "Of course. When I lived with the McCaulys, Mr. McCauly and his son George used to play every night and sometimes I'd watch them."

"So you've never actually played?" he pressed.

"No," she admitted, "but it looks simple enough."

He laughed. "I believe you were the one who said appearances can be deceiving. Have a seat and we'll see how much you learned." He pulled out a chair for her. "And don't worry, I'll go easy on you the first game or two."

That got her back up. Go easy on her, would he? She marched to the table and sat down. "Very well.

But please, don't feel you have to do less than your best on my account." She gave him a sweetly challenging smile. "Because I certainly won't."

Chapter Eight

As he set up the game, Griff pondered her shift in mood. It was as if she'd pulled back and that bothered him, but he couldn't quite put his finger on what had caused it. Going back over their conversation in his mind, they'd been discussing her taking the books with her when she moved to Tyler. Could it be that the mention of Tyler had reminded her of her plans for a fresh start, for adventure and new experiences? Was she chafing at this unexpected delay in her plans?

He'd expected her to be less eager now that she'd spent some time here at Hawk's Creek. But perhaps he'd been wrong.

He forcibly pushed his disappointment away and focused on the game. Ruby proved to be an adept player. He won the first two games, but not as easily as he'd expected. And she managed to surprise him by claiming victory in the third round.

Griff was glad to see she had a competitive streak in her. It demonstrated that there were a few thorns beneath the roses and sunshine facade she projected. And she'd need those thorns if she was going to make it on her own.

They were halfway through the fourth game when Inez interrupted them. "Here you two are. Lunch is ready."

Griff met Ruby's gaze. "Shall we continue this later? Or do you want to concede now?"

That won him an indignant glare. "From where I'm sitting, this game is still anybody's."

"Then continue later it is." He pushed his chair back, put his hands on his thighs and pushed himself up. "Inez, lead the way."

Inez didn't move immediately. "I know you usually take your meals in the dining room when we have guests, but Ruby and I have been taking our meals in the kitchen the past few days."

Griff waved Ruby on ahead of him. "If Ruby doesn't mind, then the kitchen is fine with me."

As he escorted the two women to the kitchen, Griff was surprised by how natural it felt.

A few minutes later they'd taken their seats, grace had been said and they began serving their plates.

Inez passed Ruby the bowl of butter beans. "Hard to believe that Thanksgiving is just a week from tomorrow. Are you planning to do anything special to mark the day?"

"I'm looking forward to being settled in my new living quarters in Tyler by then. I imagine there'll be a church service I can go to, and maybe there'll be some kind of community celebration."

Inez shook her head. "Sounds a mite lonely if you ask me."

"I'll have Patience and I hope to have made some friends in town by then." Ruby tried for a reassuring tone. "Besides, I'm a fairly self-sufficient person."

Griff wondered about that. Did she really think she could make it alone? A girl like her should have someone to look out for her, to ease, or even share, her burdens.

Ruby looked from one to the other of them. "How do you all celebrate Thanksgiving?"

Griff paused, not quite sure how to answer that.

Luckily, Inez chimed in first. "I always fix a nice meal, but other than that, we haven't really done much of anything to mark the day in years, not since Griff's mother died."

Ruby turned to him. "How did you celebrate when your mother was around?

He leaned back in his chair, remembering. "She and Inez used to plan a big celebration. They'd clean and decorate the house from top to bottom and recruit us kids to help."

"Not that they were very much real help," Inez interjected.

Griff flashed her an unrepentant grin before continuing. "The meal was a fabulous feast. Inez would cook for days. There'd be a pit-roasted calf and a turkey stuffed the way only Inez can. Mother would have my grandfather from Philadelphia send fresh oysters and cranberries and oranges and lots of other things we don't see around here. And there'd be more pies and sweets than people."

"You make it sound like the day was all about the food," Inez said.

Griff grinned. "For a young boy, that was the main attraction." He turned back to Ruby. "But of course it was about much more than that. We'd invite all the hands and the folks from the neighboring ranches. If the weather was nice we'd set up tables outdoors and eat under the sky. If it was too cold or wet, we'd clear all of the wagons and tools out of the barn and set up in there. After the meal, Red would play his fiddle and there'd be singing and dancing and storytelling late into the evening."

"It sounds wonderful."

The dreaminess in Ruby's voice and expression had him giving her a long look. What was with her? One minute she seemed dead set on setting out on her own and the next she seemed to have a hankering for roots.

Inez interrupted his thoughts. "You know," she said slowly, "I'm thinking it's high time we started treating Thanksgiving as a special day again."

Griff felt his brow furrow. Now what in the world had brought that on? "First time I heard you mention it."

"Oh, I've been thinking on it awhile. We don't have to do it up as fancy as we used to, at least not this year. Keep it to just Hawk's Creek folk, and of course we wouldn't need to worry about the oysters and such. After all, we don't have a lot of time to plan."

"Aren't you getting a little ahead of yourself?" Griff asked. "After all, I haven't agreed to—"

"Your mother was a fine lady and it would likely break her heart to know you and your family let the old traditions die."

She had a point. But why bring it up now, after all these years? "I suppose. Maybe we can talk to Sadie and Ry about doing something next year."

"Nonsense. Why wait an entire year when we've got seven and a half days to prepare? Besides, I wouldn't mind having an excuse to cook a fancy feast again."

Griff shook his head. "Seems like a lot of trouble for just one day."

"Griffith Michael Lassiter, just listen to yourself. Are you saying you don't have enough blessings in your life to set aside a full day to give thanks? Besides, it'll give the men something to look forward to."

Griff glanced at Ruby's face and saw a touch of longing there. And suddenly he realized Inez was right. He wasn't even sure why he'd protested in the first place. "Okay, I concede. If you want to have a big shindig, I won't stand in the way. In fact, tell me what I can do to help." And he'd find a way to get Ruby to spend it with them.

"You can invite Ry and Sadie to bring their families to join us—make it a true Lassiter Thanksgiving. It would do us all good to have this house full of young'uns again for a bit."

Ruby listened to the two of them plan their family gathering and felt another stab of jealousy. She'd prayed nightly for as long as she could remember that someday she'd have a home and a family of her own. That was another reason she'd been so eager to leave Cleebit Springs—she just couldn't see ever finding a husband there.

"What about you, Ruby?" Inez's question brought her back to the present. "You'll join us for Thanksgiving, won't you?"

Another invitation offered out of a sense of obligation? "That's very kind of you, but it sounds like this is going to be a family event and I wouldn't want to intrude."

"Nonsense, you already said you don't have anyone else to spend it with. And we'd love to have you join us, wouldn't we, Griff?"

Griff met Ruby's gaze head-on. "Of course."

"See?" Inez's voice held a that-settles-it tone. "We'd love to have you here. And I'll be insulted if you say you'd rather spend the day alone than with us."

Ruby noticed it was Inez doing all the asking. Griff only added his voice when prompted. But she'd seen something in his gaze, something that confused her. What was he truly feeling? With an effort she moved her gaze from Griff to Inez. "Really it's very kind of you, and I enjoy spending time here, but I'm eager to get started in my new life."

Inez waved a hand dismissively. "Oh, there'll be plenty of time for that after Thanksgiving."

"Might as well listen to her," Griff said with a drawl. "When Inez sets her mind to something she's like a hound who's treed a possum—she won't stop baying until you say yes."

Ruby tried to read his expression again—did he really want her to stay? Or was he just humoring Inez?

"Not a very flattering description," Inez said drily. "But accurate enough. Besides," she added, "I truly could use your help getting things ready. Lots to be done in a short amount of time."

Ruby wavered. She wouldn't want to leave Inez in the lurch if she really needed help. And the idea of meeting the other Lassiter siblings was tempting.

"You've already agreed to stay long enough for me to show you around the place," Griff added casually. "What's another few days?"

He was right. And now that she understood they were just trying to repay an imagined debt of honor, she wouldn't be in danger of mistaking it for something else. Why not take the opportunity to enjoy herself? "All right. But only if you really do let me help."

"It's a deal." Inez stabbed a chunk of carrot with her fork. "I'll send Frank to town with a telegram for Sadie and Ry."

Griff reclaimed Ruby's attention. "Is there a particular Thanksgiving tradition of yours that you'd like to include in our planning?"

She didn't have to stop and think about that one. She hadn't stayed in one place long enough to establish traditions. "Nothing special. Perhaps I can start making my own traditions once I'm truly on my own."

He looked as if he was going to question her further, but Inez spoke up first.

"If you don't mind my asking, why did you pick Tyler as your new home?"

"Like I told Griff, I don't have any family left and I wanted to start over fresh somewhere new. A big city like Tyler just seems likely to offer more opportunities for me."

Inez frowned. "But aren't you nervous about moving someplace where you don't know anyone?"

Why did everyone think this was a bad idea? "Yes, but in an excited, can't-wait-to-start kind of way. I'm not afraid, if that's what you're asking. And even if I don't know a soul there, I figure the good Lord will be watching over me and that's all I need."

Inez reached over and patted her hand. "You're right, of course. Sorry for being such an old busybody."

"Oh, I don't mind. I guess it *is* kind of unusual for a woman to strike out on her own like this."

"Actually, I did much the same when Griff's granddaddy hired me to work here. And I've never regretted it for even one minute."

Those words provided a lift to Ruby's spirit, an affirmation that she would be all right. She glanced at Griff to find him studying her, a slight frown on his face.

Inez stood. "Looks like we're all done. I'll start clearing away the dishes."

Ruby stood, as well. "I'll wash."

Griff pushed his chair back. "Since the weather's

too wet for me to do anything outdoors, I suppose I could dry."

Inez raised a brow. "Well now, those are words I never thought to hear."

Ruby looked quickly from Inez to Griff before turning to the sink. So he normally *didn't* help clean up after meals? Was he just bored today? Or did he have another reason for staying with them?

The three of them worked in companionable silence for a while. It felt nice, actually. As if they'd worked together like this for years.

Griff finally looked over his shoulder at Inez. "Since I'm back on my feet I figured I'd move back into my own room tonight. I'll get a couple of the guys to help me put mother's sitting room back to rights."

Inez tsked. "I think it might be best if you stay right where you are for now. Best not to put more strain on that foot of yours than necessary."

Griff frowned dismissively. "I can handle the stairs."

Ruby hid a smile. She could have told Inez he wasn't going to react well to that approach.

Inez, however, didn't seem willing to let the subject drop. "I'm not so sure." She cleared her throat. "By the way, did I mention that Ruby is in the guest chamber next to Sadie's old room upstairs?"

Ruby saw Griff's expression change just a few seconds before she herself realized what Inez had been trying to convey. The heat immediately climbed into her cheeks and she fumbled with the bowl she was washing. Though she trusted Griff to act honorably, and she knew Inez did as well, there were some who wouldn't think it proper for them to be the only two with bedchambers on the second floor.

"You're right," Griff said as he took the bowl from Ruby. "I think it might be best after all if I stay put for the time being. My foot is better, but there's no point pushing it too soon."

Ruby shook her head. "No, really, I can't let you give up your room for me." Her cheeks heated even more as she realized how that sounded. "I mean, I can move into the sitting room after you move upstairs. It won't be any problem at all, and I've slept in far more meager accommodations."

"Don't be ridiculous. No point shuffling everyone around." He set the drying cloth down. "Now, if you ladies can finish up in here, I need to look over some ledgers."

The rest of the day passed quietly enough. Griff stayed holed up in his office for most of the afternoon while Ruby helped Inez plan the menu and shopping list for the elaborate Thanksgiving meal. At supper they came back together and, to Ruby's relief, their interaction was relaxed and easy, just as if that earlier conversation had never happened.

Griff was pleased to see the sun shining from a clear sky the next morning. He'd had enough of being cooped up inside and not even Inez's mother-henning would deter him from riding out.

As soon as breakfast was over he turned to Ruby. "What do you say I give you that tour we discussed?"

Ruby smiled and then bit her lip. "I promised Inez I would help—"

To Griff's surprise, Inez seemed to be on his side. "Nonsense. Getting out in the fresh air will do you both a world of good."

"But—"

"No buts, young lady. I need you to keep an eye on Griff for me. If he goes gallivanting off by himself, there's no telling how he might overexert himself."

Griff spread his arms. "She's right you know. I'm not to be trusted out there on my own."

That won him a smile. "In that case," Ruby said in martyred tones, "my duty seems clear. I accept your offer."

"Good. I'll have the buckboard out front in an hour." He gave her a pointed look. "And leave the cat here."

Ruby nodded. "Of course." Then she grinned impishly. "After all, I can see you aren't ready to be climbing any more trees just yet."

He rolled his eyes at that, but refrained from comment.

"That'll give me time to pack you a picnic lunch," Inez interjected. "That way you won't have to worry about hurrying back."

Her words put Griff in mind of the previous picnic he'd shared with Ruby. And actually, thinking back on that, he'd enjoyed himself more than he'd thought he would. Even the tree-climbing incident hadn't been totally without merit. After all, it wasn't every day a man got to play the role of knight errant for a pretty girl's benefit.

Chapter Nine

Later that morning, as Griff drove the buckboard along one of the drier paths through Hawk's Creek, he decided it was time he learned a bit more about Ruby. "You mentioned you moved to Cleebit Springs when you were seven. Where did you live before that?"

She grabbed hold of the wagon seat on either side of her. "I've moved around most of my life. My ma died when I was three, and afterward, Pa just couldn't seem to settle down in one place. We lived in towns all across Kentucky, Arkansas and Louisiana before we landed in Texas."

"Then you landed in Cleebit Springs and settled down."

"Not entirely. I moved around a lot within the town. I told you before that most of the town had a hand in raising me. I lived with a number of families as I was growing up."

Did growing up that way account for her restlessness, her burning desire to move to a new place?

Was she one of those who always looked over fences, searching for greener pastures, a person who couldn't be content with what she already had? No wonder she wasn't happy with small-town life.

Which meant she'd never be happy with ranch life, either.

Now where had that thought come from?

He flicked the reins a bit more forcefully than necessary.

"Tell me about your brother and sister," she asked. "You mentioned that they're both married. Do they have children?"

"Yep, they each have a kid of their own and are helping raise another." Had leaving Hawk's Creek been worth it to them? They definitely seemed happy.

"What do you mean, raising another?"

"Ry has a foster daughter. Belle, a family friend who lived here at the ranch when we were younger, passed away a little over a year ago and named him as her daughter's guardian." Had Belle even realized that Griff had loved her? He'd never told her, and then he'd lost the chance when she fell in love with another. It had hurt more than he cared to admit when he learned she'd entrusted Ry and not him with her daughter's life. "Viola is nine years old. Then last year, Ry and his wife, Josie, had a little boy of their own. Named him Travis after my father."

"And your sister?"

"Sadie married a man from New York who moved to Texas to get a fresh start for himself and his young half sister, Penny. Penny's ten now. They also had a baby last year, a little girl they named Susannah." He smiled, remembering. "I went down to Knotty Pine to spend some time with them this past summer. Those are two of the sweetest little babies you ever want to see." Would he ever have children of his own?

"They sound like lovely people," she said. "And what a diverse family you have. I can't wait to meet them." Her expression took on a wistful cast. "You certainly have a lot to be thankful for."

She was right of course. There was no reason for him to be focused on what he didn't have. He needed to take a page from her book and do more looking for the bright side.

Griff spent the rest of the morning showing her his herds of cattle and some of his favorite spots on the place. There was the pond where he and his siblings had learned to fish, the tree where he and Ry had found a honeycomb and gotten unmercifully stung in their efforts to retrieve it, and the small meadow where his mother had liked to picnic.

Ruby seemed to take genuine delight in the tour, exclaiming over the beauty of the landmarks he pointed out or laughing at his stories. It was such a pleasure to see the ranch through fresh, *appreciative* eyes that he found himself trying to find more and more things to show her or tell her about this place he loved so much. And seeing her face light up with that warm glow when she was enjoying herself was just an added bonus.

Near noon, Griff pulled the buckboard to a stop atop a rise the family had nicknamed Hickory Hill because of the three hickory trees that dominated its crest. He often came here when he wanted to be alone, to think over some tough decision or to just enjoy the view. From here it felt as if a person could see forever.

He set the brake and turned to her. "I thought this would be a good place for us to eat that lunch Inez packed. The ground here should be a lot drier than the flatter land we just drove over."

"It's certainly a lot sunnier than our last picnic spot."

He hopped down and turned to assist her. Once her feet were on the ground, he tucked her hand on his arm rather than release it.

To keep her from stumbling, he told himself. "Before we eat, I want to show you something."

She smiled. "Your tour hasn't disappointed me yet."

He led her to the crest of the hill then waited for her reaction. A reaction that proved quite satisfactory.

"Oh, Griff, the view is breathtaking." She squeezed his arm. "I think this is my favorite place of all the ones you've shown me today." She whirled around, beaming. "But it's all been so beautiful, so alive, even in this season. I can see why you love it here so much."

Did that mean she loved it, as well? "There are spots I couldn't show you today because the ground is still so wet—wouldn't want to mire the wagon. Maybe we'll have another chance to ride out before you leave."

Her smile took on an unexpectedly shy quality.

"I'd like that very much." She removed her hand and turned back toward the wagon. "I think I'm ready for that picnic now."

When they reached the buckboard, Griff stepped ahead of her and handed her the blanket. He watched her spread the cloth in the sunniest spot she could find as he retrieved the hamper. What was she thinking? Had she reevaluated what she wanted out of life at all or did she consider all of this just a pleasant interlude on her way to something more to her liking?

And why did the answer to that seem to matter so much?

Not liking the direction his thoughts had taken, Griff set the hamper down on the cloth in front of her. When she opened it, her eyes widened. "Goodness, Inez must have thought she was feeding a half-dozen people."

He smiled. "You should know Inez by now—she doesn't do anything halfway."

She laughed outright at that and then they both dug in.

"Did you and Inez get the whole Thanksgiving Day menu planned out yesterday?" he asked as he reached for a drumstick.

"For the most part. It's definitely an ambitious undertaking. It looks as though she's planning to cook enough to feed an army."

"Like I said, Inez doesn't do anything halfway. Did she let you have much say in the planning?"

"Actually, she took quite a few of my suggestions. She's even going to let me cook one of my own favorites, venison and gingered-parsnip pie. Mrs. Tallmadge is the best cook in all of Cleebit Springs. When I lived with her family, she taught me how to cook it."

Griff considered that as he took a bite of his chicken. "You know," he said carefully, "you've mentioned living with the families of the town doctor, the midwife, the checker players, the general store owner, the encyclopedia lady and now the town's best cook. Exactly how many families did you live with growing up?"

She shifted, as if uncomfortable with his question.

"You don't have to answer if you don't want to," he said quickly.

"No, I don't mind. It's just that the truth is going to seem a bit strange to you."

He raised a brow. "All right, now I'm suitably intrigued."

Just as he'd hoped, she relaxed slightly at his teasing tone. "I told you that most of the townsfolk had a hand in raising me," she began. "I meant that literally. I moved from family to family on a regular basis."

"How so?"

"Every six months there'd be a big ceremony in town where most of the family names were put into a hat and then the preacher would draw one out. Whatever name was pulled, that's the family I'd live with for the next six months. Then, at the end of that time, we'd do it all over again."

He'd never heard of such an unusual arrangement. What had that been like? "Was it hard to live that way?"

She shrugged. "There was as much good as bad in it. One of the best things about it was, if I wasn't happy with where I was, I knew I wouldn't be there for very long."

That seemed a strange, and somewhat callous answer. Was this eagerness for new places an innate part of who she was? Or had the way she'd been brought up made her that way?

Either way, he'd do well to remember that she *was* moving on.

A flash of black-and-red caught his attention and he pointed the red-winged blackbird out to her. They watched it for a while, eating in companionable silence, until she turned to him again.

"Do you mind if I ask *you* a personal question?" she asked.

He smiled. His life was pretty much an open book. "Since I just got through prying into yours, I don't suppose it would be sporting of me to refuse."

"When you were talking about your brother and sister and their families, I could tell family was important to you. Did you never think about starting one of your own?"

He stilled, feeling sucker-punched by her question. It must have shown on his face because her cheeks reddened and she started backtracking, just as he had earlier.

"I'm sorry. I shouldn't have asked—"

"No, don't apologize. I was just surprised, is all. Yes, I've thought about it. I've just never managed to fall for a woman who loved me back."

"Oh." She started to say something else, then clamped her lips shut.

He found himself curious to know just what it was she'd started to say. "Out with it. I'm feeling expansive today so this is your one and only chance to ask your questions."

"It's just, the way you worded that answer, it made me wonder just how many women you've fallen for."

Did it now? Well, he'd opened himself up for this. "Exactly two." He started to leave it at that, but found himself expanding, almost as if compelled to do so. "I mentioned Belle to you before, the woman who left her daughter in my brother's keeping when she passed. Well, when I was younger I fancied myself in love with her. I was only sixteen at the time, and she was a couple of years older, but I made all sorts of elaborate plans about our future together. Unfortunately, I never told Belle about my feelings or my plans. She up and married a traveling preacher man."

"Oh, I'm so sorry." She clasped her hands together. "That must have been painful for you."

He shrugged, trying to downplay just how deeply it had cut. "I pined for a while like some lovesick schoolboy, but I got over it." He ran a hand through his hair. "Then I noticed Martha Davis. She was the daughter of one of the ranchers in the area and I'd known her most of my life. But the year I turned twenty, something about her caught my eye in a different way and I started courting her. I thought we were well suited—she knew all about living on a ranch and was sweet and agreeable. Then that summer she went to visit a cousin in St. Louis and decided she liked city life better than ranching. She met someone there, got married and never came back."

Griff sat back, wondering why he'd just told her all of this. She certainly hadn't asked for any details. And he'd never in all these years spoken of it to anyone.

Ruby placed a hand on his arm. "All that means is that neither of these girls was the right one for you. I'm sorry if your heart got broken, but better to find that out before you are irrevocably tied together. You just have to trust that the right person is out there, waiting for you to find her."

As if just realizing what she'd done, Ruby made as if to remove her hand, but he captured it and held it firmly in place, locking his gaze on her suddenly wide-eyed one. Had Belle and Martha broken his heart? Or just his pride? Whatever the case, telling her about his past had left him feeling lighter, freer.

He released her hand and smiled. "Enough of this gloomy talk. If you're done eating, there's one more thing I want to show you before we head back to the house."

And he'd figure out just what that was before they climbed in the buckboard. Truth to tell, he just didn't want to let this little outing end yet.

Ruby got to her knees and busied herself repacking the hamper. She hoped Griff didn't notice that her hands were a bit shaky. She could still feel the warmth and strength of his touch, the depth and intensity of his gaze.

Had something just passed between them? Or was it only her imagination? Wishful thinking perhaps?

That thought stopped her cold. What exactly was she wishing for? She'd told herself not to get too close to these people, that they were thinking of her in terms of someone who'd done them a service, and perhaps as a likable person, but nothing more.

Heavenly Father, please help me remember that he is a good man who is trying to be nice. Don't let me act the fool by thinking it's anything more.

Chapter Ten

Fifteen minutes later they were still riding across the fields. They hadn't spoken much, and the quiet seemed awkward, as if neither was sure what to say next. She was on the brink of saying something, even if it was a comment about the weather, just to break the silence, when he pulled back on the reins to stop the wagon.

Was he ready to show her another landmark?

Before she could comment, though, he raised a hand. "Did you hear that?"

There were worry lines on his brow and she wondered just what he'd heard. Straining her ears, she caught the sound of some sort of animal in distress. "What is that?"

He frowned. "It sounds like a cow bawling. Do you mind if we go check it out?"

"No, of course not."

He set the horse back in motion, turning it in the direction the sound had come from. "It's a good thing this ground is rocky here," he said, "or I'd have to walk."

She didn't say anything, just stared straight ahead, trying to get some glimpse of the animal making that distressing cry.

Of course Griff spotted the cow first. "There she is."

Ruby stared at the animal who was pacing back and forth near a tree line up ahead. "She doesn't look like she's hurt."

"No, but she's agitated and from the looks of her, her calf has missed its feeding."

Concerned, Ruby scanned the area, looking for some signs of a calf. *Please don't let the poor thing be hurt.*

When they drew closer Ruby realized the cow was on the other side of a gully from them. Griff stopped the wagon and set the brake. "The ground may be rocky, but it's still pretty messy out here. You stay put while I find out what's going on." Without waiting for her response, he jumped down and marched toward the gully's edge.

He returned quickly, his jaw set. "Her calf is down there all right. Fortunately it doesn't look hurt, but the sides are too steep and slippery for it to get itself out."

"Oh, poor thing. What do we do?"

He gave her a surprised look as he removed his jacket. "I'm going to have to drag the critter out of there. Luckily there's a rope in the back of the buckboard."

She watched as he moved around to the back and

retrieved the rope. He tied one end to the frame of the buckboard, tested it for snugness, then tossed the rest back in the wagon bed. He came around to the front and looked up at her. “I need to back the buckboard up closer to the edge of the gully. If you’ll handle the reins I’ll stand at the horse’s head. When I give the signal, release the brake, then set it again when I tell you to.”

Ten minutes later they had the buckboard positioned to his satisfaction and he’d thrown the free end of the rope down the side of the gully.

“So what now?” she asked.

“Now I go down and tie this rope around the calf and we pull him out of there.”

“Is that safe? I mean with your foot—”

He dismissed her concerns. “Other than getting good and muddy, I’ll be fine.”

“You’re sure there’s not anything I can do to help?” She felt useless just sitting here.

He studied her for a moment. “If you really want to help,” he said slowly, “there is one thing you can do.”

Ruby sat up straighter. “Just name it.”

“After I get the rope on that calf I’ll have to climb back up and direct the horse so he moves forward nice and easy. It would help if you kept an eye on the calf while I’m at the horse’s head.”

That didn’t seem like much of an assignment, but at least he was letting her help. “Sounds easy enough.”

He gave her an approving smile. "Good. Now just stay put until I climb back out."

She smiled but didn't say anything. As soon as his head disappeared over the edge, she scrambled down and moved to where she could watch him at work. He was using the rope to help in his descent and was nearly at the bottom.

As if he felt her presence, Griff looked up as soon as his feet touched bottom. Shaking his head at her as if she were a wayward child, he turned and moved toward the calf.

Ruby grinned, not at all put off by his reaction. Especially since she'd caught that hint of a smile before he'd turned away.

Watching him work, she was impressed with the confidence and quickness with which he accomplished his task. The man was clearly in his element. In almost no time at all he had the rope secured around the calf.

After a final testing of the knots, Griff quickly started back up. When he reached the top, she offered him a hand but he shook his head. "Don't want to get you muddy. I'm fine."

She stepped back and in moments he was standing back on level ground. He was breathing a bit heavier than normal and was definitely wearing some mud, but he didn't seem at all bothered by either condition. "Okay, I'm going to move to the horse's head. If you'll release the brake as soon as I'm set and then keep an eye on the calf I think we'll have this all taken care of in just a few minutes."

"Is there something I should be on the lookout for?" she asked a few moments later as she released the brake.

"The side of the gully is relatively smooth and slick so there really shouldn't be a lot of problems. Just let me know if it appears that the rope is slipping or if the calf seems to be in any sort of trouble."

She nodded and stepped back to the edge. The operation was surprisingly uneventful. Griff kept the horse moving at a steady pace and the calf eased up the gully's side with lots of bawling but little trouble. As soon as it was up and over the lip of the gully she signaled Griff, who halted the horse.

She moved closer. The calf hadn't gotten to his feet yet. Was he okay? She tentatively extended her hand. At the same time the calf lunged to his feet. Startled, Ruby took a quick step back and slipped, landing on her backside.

Griff was by her side in an instant. "Are you okay?"

She smiled. "Other than wounded dignity, I'm just fine." Seeing the look on his face, as if he'd expected her to fall to pieces over a bit of mud, she laughed outright and extended her hand. "I'm fine, really. Help me up, please?"

He took her hand and pulled her to her feet. Still slightly off balance, she stumbled forward and he caught her in his arms. He didn't step back immediately and, seeing the look in his eyes, her amusement faded, replaced by something warmer, sweeter. Oh, mercy, but having him hold her like this was so wonderful, so right, so safe. She felt as if she could face just about anything the world had to throw at her if she had *this* to fall back on when it did.

Right now she didn't give a fig whether he felt gratitude or duty or something sweeter. If he tried to kiss her, she'd let him. In fact, she'd welcome him.

Griff released her and stepped back. What was he doing? Ruby had made it abundantly clear she was eager to move to Tyler and start her new life. She was a town girl and wanted a taste of what the big city had to offer. Why did he always find himself attracted to women who had no interest in settling down on a ranch?

He turned to busy himself with untying the rope to hide his agitation. "We'd best get this fellow back to its mama so it can get some lunch."

He watched her from the corner of his eye, noting the way she stared at him with confusion and something curiously like hurt. To his relief she pulled her shoulders back and focused on his comment. "But the mother cow is on the other side of the gully. How do we get her calf to her?"

Glad to be on safe conversational ground, he pointed off to his left. "If you follow the gully for about a quarter mile that way, it narrows considerably. My pa built a bridge to span it there years ago. That's how the cow got to the other side in the first place."

She nodded. "So we just lead the calf to the bridge?"

"Something like that." He moved to the calf, lifted

it and deposited it in the bed of the buckboard. “If you don’t mind driving the wagon, I’ll ride back here and keep this little guy from jumping out.” It would also give him time to get himself back under control.

Because at the moment he wasn’t sure if his reaction back there had been the right thing to do.

Or the biggest mistake he’d ever made.

Chapter Eleven

For the next two days Ruby helped Inez get the house ready for Thanksgiving, while Griff declared himself well enough to resume his regular routine. The three of them still got together at mealtimes and Ruby enjoyed listening to Griff talk about his day. What she enjoyed even more were his and Inez's efforts to include her. She wasn't used to people asking for her opinion or listening so intently to what she had to say.

During the midday meal on Friday, a telegraph arrived informing them that both Ry's and Sadie's families had accepted the invitation to return to Hawk's Creek for Thanksgiving. From Griff and Inez's response to the news, Ruby realized neither had been as certain as they pretended they were that Griff's siblings would come. She caught Inez actually humming that afternoon as they were polishing the woodwork in the front hall.

The evenings were becoming Ruby's favorite time of the day. After the supper chores were taken care of, she would take Patience and curl up in the study with one of the books Griff had selected for her and get happily lost in the world of the story. After about an hour or so, Griff would join her and challenge her to a game of checkers.

And while the competition between them was fun, what she really enjoyed were their discussions. He would ask her questions about the book she'd been reading, giving his own opinions on the passages he remembered. They didn't always agree on the finer points, but the debates they had were invigorating rather than confrontational.

On Saturday evening she noticed that even Patience had softened toward Griff. The cat drifted over while they were playing checkers, but rather than approach her, she began stropping herself against one of Griff's legs, purring softly. Even more surprising, Griff absently reached down and stroked the animal as he pondered his next move. Ruby hid a smile, wondering if her opponent was even aware of what he was doing. Apparently he wasn't as averse to cats as he'd claimed.

Strange to think that she'd only known Griff Lassiter for a week and a day. So much about her life had changed in that short time. Even her ideas about what life could be, and of her place in it, had shifted slightly.

There were no more encounters like the ones they'd shared during their outing on Thursday. She was beginning to believe any emotion on his part other than solicitousness had come purely from her imagination.

And she told herself she could be content with his friendship. After all, she'd had very few friends in her life.

On Sunday Ruby attended church service with Griff and Inez. It was sweet and somehow affirming to have Griff introduce her to his friends and neighbors as a family friend.

She met Reverend Martin and his wife, Olivia. The elderly couple seemed very nice and it hit Ruby as she spoke to them that if things had gone differently last week she would have spent that first night away from Cleebit Springs with them instead of at Hawk's Creek. Had that happened, she would have never met Inez, might never have seen Griff again.

Thank You, Father, for setting me on that frightening but oh-so-rewarding path. My life has been made so much richer because of it.

Later, after lunch, Ruby watched as Griff pushed away from the table and carried his dishes to the sink.

"The weather's been cooperating lately and the ground has dried out considerably," he said, meeting her gaze. "What do you say I give you the second half of that tour?"

Ruby felt her spirits lift. "Oh, that would be lovely." Then she turned to Inez. "After I help with the dishes, of course."

But Inez waved her offer aside. "You two go on and leave this to me." She shook a finger at them. "But I expect you to take care of the supper dishes without me tonight."

Before Ruby could say anything, Griff grinned.

"It's a deal." Then he turned to her. "How do you feel about riding horseback?"

She smiled. "I enjoy it, but I haven't ridden in a while." Her father had taught her to ride when she was quite young, but opportunities to ride had been hit or miss since—depending on what family she'd lived with.

"I'll have Mabel saddled up for you, then. She's gentle but not a plodder."

An hour and a half later they had ridden through a wooded area to visit a spot where he and his brother had built a fort out of old lumber, they'd skirted the edge of a pond that had a picturesque stair-step waterfall feeding it and had collected a couple dozen ripe persimmons to bring back to Inez.

Ruby was learning to love Hawk's Creek more and more with each new discovery. Seeing it through Griff's eyes made it doubly precious. She could see clearly now what a part of him this place was. Take him away from here for any great length of time and his spirit, the part of him that made him uniquely Griff, would shrivel like an uprooted plant.

Griff watched the appreciation and delight shine in Ruby's face as she discovered the parts that made up the whole of Hawk's Creek. And it wasn't just the places he showed her. She took pleasure in pointing things out to him as well—like the pair of deer she spotted bounding across a corner of an open field before disappearing into a stand of trees, a large rock formation that she decided looked just like a snail and a hawk circling high above them.

It was so easy to see her in this world.

Only this wasn't the world she seemed to want. But why not? If her life to this point had been so filled with sunshine and butterflies, why did she feel the need to move to a big city where she could lose herself in the anonymity of crowds?

It suddenly seemed important to him to find out.

He led them to a nearby spot that he knew would be perfect for having such a discussion. It was near the tree line so was somewhat sheltered, but open enough that it would be filled with warming sunshine this time of day. There were several large rocks strewn about so there would be dry places to sit. And a stream ran through it, so the sound of gurgling water would provide a serene backdrop. She'd love it.

Sure enough, as soon as the clearing came into sight she gave a little coo of delight. "Oh, Griff, this is lovely."

"Why don't we get down and let the horses drink and graze for a while."

"I'd like that."

They strolled around for a bit, drank water from the stream from cupped hands and talked about the upcoming Thanksgiving feast. Almost by mutual consent they sat on a large rock, and faced the stream.

"It's like a sofa, hand-carved by God for our comfort," she mused, "and set in the middle of the most beautiful sitting room in the world."

Griff leaned back, bracing his weight on his palms.

"You have the most fanciful way of looking at the world," he said with a smile.

She shrugged. "It's just as easy to look for the good as the bad in things. And much more productive. My dad taught me that."

That gave him an opening and he took it. "You told me your dad passed away when you were seven. What happened to him?"

She stiffened and her expression went blank. "I'd rather not talk about that."

Whatever had happened, it must have been traumatic. "Had he been ill?"

She shook her head and dug around on the ground for some pebbles, which she began pitching one at a time into the stream.

He should drop this and respect her privacy. But something about her closed-off expression, about the set of her jaw and the tremble of her hands whispered to him that perhaps she needed to talk about this, whatever *this* was.

"So I take it your father's demise is the only wrinkle in your otherwise perfect life."

Her head whipped around and she stared at him with something akin to fury in her eyes. "My *perfect* life. Is that what you think? You have no idea—" Her lips snapped shut.

"Because you haven't told me anything but the good. Yes, you were orphaned at seven and that is a terrible thing for a young child. But it happens to many children. And you had a whole town full of people ready to step in and take care of you. You grew up knowing that you would always have someone looking out for you."

"Those people didn't want to take care of me, no matter how useful I tried to make myself. They did it out of guilt and obligation. That name-drawing ceremony every six months that I told you about—the family whose name was selected considered it a misfortune, not a blessing." She took a deep breath. "I even learned recently that those who didn't 'win' the drawing were obliged to pay a small amount into an account for my future. And most preferred to do that."

Her voice had risen and her expression shouted at him to drop the subject. But he had to see this through now. "For someone who always tries to see the bright side of things, you are sure giving this a dark turn. Perhaps the townsfolk weren't all vying for the privilege of looking after you. But even if they were making the best of what they saw as a bad situation and trying to spread the burden, they still stood by you and saw that you were taken care of. That has to show some measure of concern."

She glared at him, her hands balled up into tight fists. "You want to know about my life? Okay, here's my story."

Griff settled back, satisfied. Perhaps now he'd understand what made her tick just a little better.

"I told you how my pa couldn't seem to be happy staying in any one place for very long after my mother passed," she began. "Well, that summer I turned seven we were traveling through the Texas backwoods and got lost. It wasn't the first time that happened and

Pa usually made a game out of it, calling it a grand adventure. We traveled in a buckboard with several days' worth of supplies and we'd slept in it or on the ground lots of times before. But during the second day of that grand adventure the wagon broke down and we were forced to ride double on the wagon horse while we looked for help."

Griff didn't like the way this story was going. Ruby might have thought the world of her father, but to his reckoning it didn't sound as if the man had given much thought to his daughter's welfare.

"Only we weren't looking all that hard," she continued. "We'd found a small lake where we could swim and fish, and were having a wonderful time camping there. Then, the third night we were there, we heard a group of men approaching our camp on horseback. Pa told me to go hide behind a nearby tree and to not come out until he told me it was safe."

At least the man had had that much sense. Then he realized Ruby had started shaking and her expression was a mask of despair. What had happened that night? Whatever it was, reliving it seemed too much for her. Perhaps this hadn't been such a good idea after all. "Ruby, I'm sorry I pressed you. You don't have to—"

"Yes, I do." She swallowed. "To make a long story short, those men were from Cleebit Springs. They were hunting down a thief who'd come through town and robbed and killed a well-loved matriarch. When they stumbled on my father, they decided he was the guilty party."

Chapter Twelve

Griff's pulse kicked up as he realized some of the horror that was to come for her. But he held his peace, realizing that perhaps she really *did* need to get through this recounting of her personal nightmare.

"I heard all the yelling and cursing and I was scared, but I stayed hidden like my pa had told me. When I finally couldn't stand not knowing what was happening any longer, I peeked out from behind the tree." She swallowed hard and he could tell she was no longer with him. She was that frightened little girl deep in the East Texas backwoods again. He squeezed her hand, trying to anchor her to the here and now. To make certain she knew she wasn't alone this time.

"My father was hanging from the very tree we'd slept under the night before. I was just in time to see the last feeble jerk of his body before he went still."

Griff felt the shock of that revelation slam him in the gut and the gorge rise in his throat. She'd only been seven years old.

She shivered. “I don’t remember much of that night after that—just screaming and screaming until my voice wouldn’t work anymore.”

He stroked her hair, wishing he could take that pain from her, could pluck those ugly memories from her mind. But she wasn’t finished talking.

“Two days later they found the man who had actually committed the crime. They say he looked a lot like my pa, though I never saw him myself. That’s when Pastor Hannaly exhorted them all for the sin they had committed and told them it was their Christian duty to see that I was looked after the way my father would have wanted. Since no one family wanted to take responsibility, they came up with the taking-turns system.”

There were tears running down her cheeks, but he didn’t think she was aware of them. “Oh, Ruby, I’m so sorry you had to go through that. Now that I know, it’s even more amazing to me what a sweet, strong, generous person you turned out to be.”

She didn’t appear to have heard him. “The thing is, no one likes living with a reminder of the sins they’ve committed. No matter how docile I was, how much in the background I tried to stay, all I saw when they looked at me was guilt and resentment.”

A sob escaped her and she tried to smile. “Sorry. I know you don’t like crying females.”

Griff put a finger to her lip. “Don’t apologize.” He pulled her to him, hugging her against his chest as he stroked her hair. “You have a right to cry. Sob to your heart’s content—no one will hear you but me.”

And cry she did—heartrending sobs that seemed to come from the very center of her being. Sobs that shook her and wouldn't let her go.

Griff held her close, whispering soothing words, rocking her in his arms, gently rubbing her back. And berating himself roundly. How many times had he thought her shallow or selfish for wanting to leave Cleebit Springs when she had so many "friends" there? He'd even told her at one point that she was lucky to have such a large foster family. What a self-righteous fool he'd been. He could only imagine how his words must have hurt her. If there was any way at all he could make it up to her, he would.

Finally her crying tapered off, her body stilled its shaking and she went limp in his arms.

"I'm so sorry," she said, her voice muffled against his chest.

"I'm not."

She looked up at that. "I've gotten your shirt all damp and mussed."

"It'll dry." He stroked her hair, loving the soft-as-a-kitten feel of it. "I think you needed that. I'm just glad I could be here to hold you while you got it out."

She stared into his eyes with a watery smile. "I think you must be the kindest person in the whole world."

Is that how she saw him? As a *kind* person? That was something you said about a friend. And he suddenly wanted to be so much more to her.

Griff placed a hand against her cheek, then slowly

traced the line of her jaw. "And you must be the loveliest—in every sense of that word."

Her eyes darkened and he heard a little catch in her breathing. Slowly he lowered his head, longing to kiss her but giving her the chance to protest if he was alone in that desire.

But there was no sign of protest, no pulling back. Instead she raised her face and her eyes fluttered closed. That was all the invitation Griff needed.

He dipped his head and kissed her.

He'd promised himself to keep it brief, chaste, that he would only be offering her comfort and affirmation. But when her hand snaked around his neck and she pressed closer, those good intentions went out the window. He deepened the kiss, suddenly wanting to let her know that she would never have to face those memories alone again as long as he was with her. He wanted to let her know that she was cherished and admired and...and what?

When he finally raised his head, Griff felt stunned by the force of the emotions stampeding through him. The only explanation was that he was in love with Ruby. How had this happened? *When* had this happened?

The need to protect her from further hurt, to keep her always safe, and always by his side was almost overwhelming.

Staring down at her he was pleased to note she looked equally stunned. The wonder in her eyes as she stared at him, the softness of her smile, brought out all of his protective urges. There wasn't anything she could have asked of him at that moment that he wouldn't have attempted to do for her. And after the way she'd reacted to the ranch, he had reason to hope she could be happy here.

But he had to take it slow, had to woo her properly. She deserved that.

So he stood and reached down his hands to help her up. "It's getting late. Time to head back to the house."

She dusted off the back of her skirt and then let him help her mount, that shy softness still shimmering around her.

Griff climbed up on Chester, feeling pretty pleased with the world in general. All in all it had been quite a productive day.

As they started off, Griff set their pace to a comfortable walk and pulled his horse alongside hers. "We'll take a more direct route back to the house than the one we took when we headed out," he told her. "We should be there in twenty minutes or so."

She nodded and they rode in companionable silence for a while, though he caught her watching him from time to time.

"It's getting a mite chilly out here. What say when we get back to the house, I fix us both up a big cup of hot chocolate?"

"You're being much too nice to me."

"Nothing's too good for the woman who saved my life." He'd almost said *the woman I love.*

Moving slowly was going to be a whole lot harder than he imagined.

* * *

Ruby's smile froze as his words sunk in. Is that how he thought of her—as the woman who'd saved his life? Nothing more personal? After that kiss, she'd thought—fool!

She nudged her horse into a fast trot, wanting an excuse not to talk, not to make eye contact. A moment ago she'd felt herself the luckiest woman on earth. She'd dared to believe that Griff, a man who'd come to mean more to her than she'd ever dreamed possible, might really love her. She'd opened herself up for the first time in thirteen years, shared all her ugly, painful memories, and he'd treated that pain with a gentleness and respect that had touched her deeply.

And then that kiss—she'd never felt so safe and warm and truly *loved* in her life.

And it had all been done out of a need to repay her, and perhaps a touch of pity.

The soaring happiness she'd felt a moment ago shattered around her in a thousand needle-sharp pieces. And there was no one but herself to blame. She'd known from the outset how it was, had warned her heart not to forget it. But she *had* forgotten and it had cost her dearly. Because she'd given him her heart and it was too late to get it back.

Somehow she got through the rest of the day, finding reasons not to be alone with Griff. After supper she claimed a headache—no pretense there—and went to bed early.

Not that she got much sleep. Staring at the darkened ceiling, she came to a painful but necessary decision in the wee hours before dawn.

Chapter Thirteen

The next morning, as soon as Griff rode out, Ruby faced Inez. "I have decided to leave for Tyler today."

Inez stilled, her expression sobering. "May I ask why?"

Ruby waved a hand, as if waving away any arguments to her decision. "It's best this way. Putting off my leaving will not make it any easier and it's probably best if I don't insert myself into a family gathering."

"You know that to me and Griff you are family."

Inez's simple words were almost Ruby's undoing. But she managed to hold herself together. "That's a very kind thing to say, but at best I am a family friend. And please believe that I will always consider myself your friend."

Inez took a step forward and touched Ruby's arm. "Whatever happened between you and Griff, I'm sure—"

Ruby stepped back, afraid she would shatter at

the next touch. "Please. I've made up my mind." She pulled an envelope from her pocket and set it on the counter. "Would you give this to Griff when he returns?"

"Of course." Inez's shoulders slumped. "Will you at least let me send someone to town with you? Griff will want to know that you arrived safely and have found accommodations."

Ruby wavered for a minute. She'd rather not take anything else from them, but Inez was right. If she didn't accept an escort, Griff would no doubt feel obligated to ride after her and make certain she was okay. "Thank you, that's very thoughtful of you."

Thirty minutes later, Ruby was passing underneath the wrought-iron arch that guarded the entrance to Hawk's Creek, Archie riding on a horse ahead of her. The sudden thought that this was likely the very last time she would pass this way was enough to bring a lump to her throat.

She reached down and stroked Patience's head. "It's just you and me again," she said thickly. "But don't you worry, things are going to work out just fine. Spending Thanksgiving at Hawk's Creek would have been a mistake—we'd have been comparing every other Thanksgiving to that one from then on."

But she wondered who she was trying to convince, Patience or herself? Because whether she attended the Thanksgiving festivities or not, she had a feeling deep inside that she'd be comparing every home she ever lived in from here on out to the one she'd experienced briefly there at Hawk's Creek.

* * *

"What do you mean, she's gone?" Griff stared at Inez as if she'd gone mad. There had to be some mistake.

"She left first thing this morning. I sent Archie with her. He should be back soon."

"Why'd you let her go?"

"This isn't a prison. She's free to go whenever she wants." Inez snatched an envelope off the counter and handed it to him. "Here. She left this for you."

A note.

Griff sat down at the table and tore it open.

Griff,

Thank you so much for all the kindness and hospitality you've shown me the past few days. Your efforts to repay me for the small service I did for you were most gratefully received and meant more to me than you will ever know. Spending time at Hawk's Creek has left me with some of the happiest memories of my life. It was the perfect way to begin my fresh-start adventure.

I know I agreed to spend Thanksgiving with you and your family, but I have decided that it really would be best for me to start my new life right away. I hope you will forgive me for leaving without saying goodbye, but I feared you would try to talk me out of this and I am not sure I could have withstood your very considerable powers of persuasion, especially when you are determined to be generous.

Please don't feel obligated to follow me to try to change my mind. You won't succeed and it will only be awkward for both of us. I hope that whenever you have occasion to be in Tyler, though, that you will look me up to say hello.

I do truly wish you every happiness.

Yours, always

Ruby Tuggle

P.S. I took you up on your generous offer to lend me some of your books. Rest assured I will take very good care of them until such time as you should come to collect them.

Griff scanned it a second time, trying to read between the lines and understand what she'd been attempting to convey. Unfortunately, the truth seemed clear. Despite everything, she still wanted to start that new life in Tyler.

How could he have been so foolish? Apparently he'd read something into that kiss they'd shared that just hadn't been there. He should have realized. She'd just been through a very draining experience, had relived the most awful day of her life and then cried until his shirt was drenched with her tears. It had been reaction to that emotional turmoil, nothing more.

She didn't love him, at least not enough to give up her dreams for him.

He should be used to this by now—after all, he'd been through it before.

Except he hadn't. What he'd felt for Belle and Martha had been schoolboy fancies—he realized that now. He'd been taken with the *idea* of being in love and so had decided that's what he felt. But those feelings had been mere shadows of emotion compared to what he felt for Ruby.

"Griff." Inez's voice cut across his jumbled thoughts. "I don't know what she says in that note, or what passed between you to make her feel she had to leave, but I do know that she loves you. I see it every time she looks at you. The same way I see your feelings when you look at her."

"You're wrong. She wanted her life in the city more." He stood. "I'll be working on putting Mother's sitting room back to rights. Let me know when Archie gets back."

He marched out of the room without waiting for a response. He needed to be alone to work off some of this raging drive to follow her. Moving furniture was just the ticket.

There was no one to blame in this mess but himself. She'd been oppressively tied to Cleebit Springs, to people who wished her elsewhere, for most of her life. If being on her own with room to breathe and a future that was hers alone to chart was what she needed, then he wouldn't stand in her way, even if it strangled something deep inside him.

The next day Griff worked himself until he was drenched in sweat and too tired and sore to do more than eat and go to bed. Archie had assured him that

Ruby had secured a room in a genteel boardinghouse in one of the nicer parts of Tyler. That had alleviated one of his worries, but he still lay awake most of the night wondering how she was faring being truly on her own for the first time in her life.

Sadie and Ry and their families arrived on Wednesday and Griff tried to put aside his roiling thoughts to give them the welcome they expected and deserved. And it *was* good to have everyone at Hawk's Creek again. Inez had been right—it had been much too long since they'd had a proper family gathering.

The only problem was, for him, there was an important someone missing.

He'd thought he was doing a good job of hiding his unfocused and generally gloomy thoughts, though, until that evening when he stepped out on the front porch to be alone for a minute. Within moments Sadie had followed him.

"All right, brother mine, let's hear it."

"Hear what?"

"Whatever it is that has you in this pensive mood. Is there something wrong with the ranch operations?"

"No. Everything here is just fine."

"Then it's something else." She stared at him a moment, then smiled. "Could it be lady troubles? Oh, Griff, have you finally found your true love?"

Griff rolled his eyes. "Now you sound like a fairy tale."

"That's not an answer."

He turned and leaned against the porch rail, trying

to keep Sadie from seeing how close to the mark she'd hit. "Don't you have a daughter to see to?"

"Mercy me, it *is* a girl." Sadie joined him at the rail, practically bouncing on her toes. "Who is she and when can I meet her?"

"It's no one you know and you won't be meeting her." He looked out over the front lawn, wondering what Ruby was doing this Thanksgiving eve. "She doesn't feel the same about me," he added reluctantly.

Sadie stilled. "Are you sure?"

"She as much as told me so."

"What's that you have in your pocket? Did she write you a letter?"

Griff realized he must have unconsciously patted his pocket when he answered her. Like a lovesick fool, he'd been carrying Ruby's letter with him, pulling it out to read periodically, trying to figure out how he could have read the woman herself so wrong.

"Can I read it?"

He glared down at her. "It's private."

She kept her hand out. "I thought you might want a woman's perspective on what she wrote."

He started to refuse her again, then found himself pulling the note from his pocket. She'd just keep nagging until he showed it to her, he told himself. Yet a little voice in his head kept whispering that perhaps she *would* see something he'd missed.

Sadie read the letter through and then read it again, finally looking back up at him, a smug smile on her face. "Oh, yes, she definitely loves you."

Griff's pulse kicked up a notch but he knew it was

just a false hope. "Thanks for the nice try, Sadie girl, but you can't possibly—"

"Of course I can. The way she talks about your *powers of persuasion* and her pleas for you to not follow her, that's a girl who knows she can't say no to you. The statement that her time at Hawk's Creek left her with happy memories, the regret over leaving without saying goodbye and the hope that you'll visit her, all speak to her deep affection for you. And her closing—*Yours, always*—my goodness Griff, can the girl be any clearer than that?"

"I'd like to believe you, but then why did she leave when we gave her every encouragement to stay?"

"You must have done something to send her running."

That's what he kept telling himself. But for the life of him he couldn't figure out just what it had been.

"Tell me a little about her and how you met," Sadie urged. "She mentions a small service she did for you?"

"I was escorting her to Cornerstone from a town about a days' ride from here when I got sick along the way—coughing, high fever, couldn't stay upright to get home under my own power. She got me here and helped Inez tend to me until I got better."

"Oh, my, that's some small service."

"Exactly. She's rather amazingly generous and spirited."

"And you fell in love with her."

How was it his little sister was making him feel like a schoolboy and she was the teacher? "I did."

"But did you tell her?"

"No. I mean, I only just realized it a few days ago myself. And we'd only known each other a little over a week. I thought it best to go slowly."

Sadie shook her head in disgust. "Men." She raised a brow. "I suppose you did manage to tell her, though, just how grateful you were for all her help."

"Of course."

"I thought so." She held up Ruby's letter. "It's all here, plain as day."

"What's all there?"

"Look at this." She began reading random snippets from the letter. *"Thank you so much for all the kindness and generosity...your efforts to repay me...when you are determined to be generous...please don't feel obligated."*

"So?"

"She thinks you feel gratitude, not love. Though why that should send her scurrying—"

"Not gratitude." Griff felt as though the fog was beginning to part. It was *obligation* she saw in his actions, the kind of oppressive, resentful sense of obligation from others that had haunted her life for years. No wonder she'd left him.

"No?" Sadie sounded deflated.

Griff grabbed her by the shoulder and gave her a resounding kiss on the cheek. "Sadie, my girl, you are the best sister a fellow could ask for."

"Of course I am. But what did I do?"

"You just gave me a reason to hope."

Chapter Fourteen

Ruby looked at the stack of books on her bedside table. Which one would she read today?

Spending a day lost in the pages of a book was something she'd often dreamed about, and now she had that chance. She couldn't help but feel a little tug of longing, though, when she thought of how she had planned to spend Thanksgiving just a few days ago.

Griff's family would all be at the ranch by now. And Inez would have most of the feast prepared with just a few last-minute items still cooking. Would Inez even remember the venison and gingered-parsnip pie Ruby had planned to make? Not that it mattered—there would be more than enough food without it.

Sunshine streamed in through her window, which meant the tables would be set out on the side lawn at Hawk's Creek rather than in the barn.

She glanced at Patience, curled up on the coverlet of her bed. "As soon as it warms up a bit outside we'll go for a walk. I promise."

Before Ruby could open her book, someone knocked at her door. She looked at her clock—just a few minutes after seven. Mighty early for callers. Especially since she didn't know anyone here.

Ruby opened the door to find Miss Bermont, the boardinghouse proprietor, standing there with a frown on her face.

"Can I help you?" Ruby asked.

"You have a visitor." The woman lifted her chin. "It is quite early in the day for visitors, especially *gentleman* visitors."

Ruby's pulse quickened. She could only think of one person who would come calling. But he'd have had to set out before breakfast… "Did he give a name?"

"Mr. Lassiter."

Why had he come when she'd asked him not to? She should send him away. But, oh, she did so want to see him.

"Well? Should I send him on his way?"

What if it wasn't what she thought? What if Inez needed her for something? She'd never know if she didn't see him. "Please tell him I'll be right down."

Miss Bermont pursed her lips disapprovingly, but nodded. "Very well. But please see that you leave the parlor door open while you are entertaining guests. I run a reputable house here."

"Of course." Ruby moved to the vanity and checked her appearance, fluffing her hair with hands that shook slightly. She moved to the door, then, deciding it might be a good idea to have something to hold on to, turned and picked up her cat. Then she hurried from the room before her courage failed her.

Reaching the parlor door, she took a deep, steadying breath, then entered with a smile. "Mr. Lassiter, how nice to see you again."

"Hello, Ruby."

He stood there, hat in hand smiling at her, and her knees nearly buckled. The look in his eyes, the warmth of his tone left her breathless and warm and wanting. Oh, but she had it bad. She loved him. Truly, deeply loved him.

And something inside of her was breaking all over again at the thought that he didn't return the feeling.

Trying to get herself back under control, Ruby bypassed the settee and took a seat on one of the high-backed chairs. "Did your family make the trip okay?" she asked, thankful that Patience was tolerating her lap.

"They did. All eight of them arrived yesterday and the house is ringing with their voices. But I didn't come here to talk about them."

She was too much of a coward to ask what he *had* come here to talk about. Instead she nervously tried to fill the pauses. "Shouldn't you be back at Hawk's Creek, celebrating Thanksgiving with all of them?"

"I have something I need to take care of first."

"Oh?" Was he here running errands and had just stopped by to say hello? She wasn't sure how much more of this she could stand. Yet she didn't want to see him leave, either.

He moved to stand directly in front of her. "Yes. I need to tell you that I love you."

Ruby's hand stilled on the cat's back and she stared up at him, afraid she'd misunderstood. "What did you say?"

He knelt down in front of her. "I said I love you. I don't feel merely obliged, or grateful or honor-bound. I love you, deeply, completely, madly. And I couldn't bear to go another day without making certain you knew it."

"But…but you hardly know me."

"On the contrary, I know you are incredibly generous, and forgiving and strong in ways that humble me. You have spirit and a joyful heart that not even the darkest of circumstances could dim. And I know that you are the one person who makes me feel complete. So you see, I know everything about you that matters. As for the rest, it would be my great pleasure to take the remainder of my life discovering your other qualities."

Was he actually proposing? "Oh, Griff, I do so love you." She let Patience jump down and leaned forward to place a hand on his chest. "I think I began falling for you the first time we met, when you stooped to help me with the dropped dishes." She laughed, a laugh that ended on a sob of happiness. "Your heroic rescue of Patience just sealed the deal."

Griff gathered her up in his arms and gave her a kiss that rivaled that first one they'd shared. When he was done, he tapped her nose. "Now, while I still have a shred of self-control left, go and get your things. We have a Thanksgiving celebration to attend."

She stood, and moved to the door on feet that had wings.

"And Ruby," he called after her, "I mean all of your things. You won't be returning here—you're coming home."

Chapter Fifteen

Griff sat at the head of the long table set out under the clear blue sky. The boards literally sagged under the weight of all the food Inez had prepared. Family and near-family lined both sides.

Ruby sat to his right, glowing with happiness. He still couldn't believe he'd almost let her get away from him. He wouldn't make that mistake again. She'd agreed to marry him and as far as he was concerned, the sooner the better. His family had taken to her just as he'd known they would. Already she and Sadie and Josie were becoming fast friends.

Sadie and her family sat next to Ruby with little Susannah perched on his sister's lap, happily shaking a silver rattle. When she wasn't gumming it, anyway. Eli was whispering something in Sadie's ear, while Penny leaned across the table, talking to Viola.

Ry sat to his left. Ry bounced baby Travis on his knee, trying to distract him from reaching down to grab Patience's tail. Josie, not so hindered as her son, had filched a bit of something from the table and was surreptitiously feeding it to the always-hungry feline. Viola's cat, Daffy, caught sight of them and was making a beeline their way.

On the other end of the table, his Hawk's Creek family, Inez, Red and the others, were just settling into their places.

Griff stood and immediately everyone quieted and gave him their attention. "God has been mighty good to me this year, as I'm sure He's been to all of you, as well. Today being Thanksgiving, I thought it only right we all take turns in sharing some of the things we're thankful for."

He looked around the table. "The things I'm most thankful for are all of you gathered here. For my family, by both birth and marriage, whose love for each other and for me is a true blessing, and who have brought extra joy to all of us by ushering this new generation of cousins into the world. For Inez, who has been like a surrogate mother to us Lassiters, and who encouraged me to renew this tradition of gathering with family and friends to remember how truly blessed we are. May it be the first of many such gatherings to come."

He waited for the general chorus of *Hear, hear!* to die down before he continued. "I'm also thankful for the rest of my Hawk's Creek family, who have stood by me through times of plenty and of want, of drought and flood, ensuring that this place we all love remains strong."

Then he turned to Ruby. "Last, but in no way least,

I will get down on my knees every morning and every night and thank God for sending Miss Ruby Anne Tuggle into my life."

He tugged on her hand and drew her up beside him. "Just a few moments ago, Ruby and I had a little talk. We'd like you to all know that you are invited to return here for a Christmas Eve wedding."

Cheers and exclamations erupted from those at the table and most everyone got to their feet to shake Griff's hand and welcome Ruby into the family.

Through it all, Griff kept a firm hold on Ruby's hand, loving the way it fit so perfectly in his. And he said a silent prayer of Thanksgiving, thanking God for sending him this amazing woman who so generously returned his love.

The two of them together, today and always, would see that their home at Hawk's Creek would always be one of love and thanksgiving.

* * * * *

Dear Reader,

Griff is the final sibling in the Lassiters of Hawks' Creek family to get a story of his own and in many ways his was the most difficult to write. Throughout the other books in this series, he remained enigmatic. Extremely taciturn, not only was he tight-lipped when it came to dialogue, but he was also very stubborn about letting me in on his thoughts and backstory. I knew Griff had some hurtful secrets in his past, but it wasn't until I introduced him to Ruby Anne Tuggle that I began to get some idea as to just what those secrets might be.

As for Ruby, my goodness but that girl came bursting onto the scene with one of the most complex and interesting backstories of any character I've ever had the privilege to write about. And though she was young, a bit of a Pollyanna and as purposefully optimistic as Griff was dour, she proved to be his perfect match.

I hope you enjoyed reading about Griff and Ruby's rocky journey to their happily-ever-after as much as I enjoyed writing it.

Wishing you much love and blessings in your life,

Winnie

Questions for Discussion

1. Do you think Ruby initially approached Griff simply because he was her only choice of an escort, or was there more to it than that? Why do you think this?

2. Did Griff's agreement to provide escort for a young woman who was a virtual stranger to him ring true to you? Why or why not?

3. Why do you think Ruby was so attached to her cat, Patience?

4. Do you think Griff was merely being stubborn by refusing to admit he was too sick for travel, or that he was truly unaware of how sick he was? What makes you feel that way?

5. What role do you think Inez played in helping Griff and Ruby work through their issues?

6. Given that she seemed eager to start living her new life, why do you think Ruby was willing to keep delaying her departure from Hawk's Creek?

7. What changes did you note in Griff and in his feelings toward Ruby once he learned the truth of how she came to live in Cleebit Springs?

8. Did the conversation between Griff and his sister, Sadie, ring true to you? Have you ever had a similar conversation with a sibling or close friend that led to a radical shift in your understanding of a troubling situation?